**Indulge yourself with this powerful new duet
from bestselling author Caroline Anderson!**

The Legendary Walker Doctors

Two of the medical profession's finest—
the broodingly gorgeous and *exceptionally* talented
twin brothers Ben and Matt Walker—have arrived
in the town of Yoxburgh, leaving a trail of
fluttering female hearts in their wake!

But Ben and Matt must go above and beyond to
prove their love to the two women they *actually* want...

In Book One, find out how baby doctor and doting dad
Ben convinces neighbour Daisy to risk her heart on him
and his daughter in **TEMPTED BY DR DAISY!**

In Book Two, **THE FIANCÉE HE CAN'T FORGET**,
obstetrician Matt persuades ex-fiancée Amy to let him
back into her life—but will she let him into her heart?

Both titles are available this month.

Also available from www.millsandboon.co.uk

THE FIANCÉE
HE CAN'T FORGET

BY
CAROLINE ANDERSON

MILLS & BOON

First published in Great Britain 2011
by Mills & Boon, an imprint of Harlequin (UK) Limited.
Harlequin (UK) Limited, Eton House, 18-24 Paradise Road,
Richmond, Surrey TW9 1SR

© Caroline Anderson 2011

ISBN: 978 0 263 21918 0

Dear Reader,

When I was asked to write a duet of two closely linked books, I thought 'How close can people be?' And the answer? Identical twins who are both gorgeous guys and amazing doctors—my LEGENDARY WALKER DOCTORS. But they're not just normal twins, but twins who'd shared the same amniotic sac, who'd been in touch with each other from the first moment and who now, 34 years later, were still very close emotionally and in their working lives. You really can't get closer than that—and for both Ben and Matt, their journeys have been paved with tragedy and pain.

But then Ben moves to Yoxburgh, where Daisy and Amy, dear friends and colleagues, are waiting in the wings.

Ben has a daughter, little Florence, who is the centre of his world—until he meets Daisy. He just has to find a way for both of them to trust again, so together they can give Florence the family they all long for in TEMPTED BY DR DAISY.

For Matt and Amy, the past is so painful they can't bear to go there again, but when Ben and Daisy fall in love, her best friend and his twin are brought together again and circumstances conspire to force them to face their past and deal with the loss that drove them apart in THE FIANCÉE HE CAN'T FORGET.

Writing their stories was heart-wrenching but wonderful, and I hope you enjoy reading them as much as I enjoyed coaxing them along each step of the way.

With love,

Caroline

Caroline Anderson has the mind of a butterfly. She's been a nurse, a secretary, a teacher, run her own soft-furnishing business, and now she's settled on writing. She says, 'I was looking for that elusive something. I finally realised it was variety, and now I have it in abundance. Every book brings new horizons and new friends, and in between books I have learned to be a juggler. My teacher husband John and I have two beautiful and talented daughters, Sarah and Hannah, umpteen pets, and several acres of Suffolk that nature tries to reclaim every time we turn our backs!' Caroline also writes for Mills & Boon® Cherish™.

Recent titles by the same author:

Medical™ Romance
ST PIRAN'S: WEDDING OF THE YEAR
THE SURGEON'S MIRACLE
THE VALTIERI MARRIAGE DEAL

Mills & Boon® Cherish™
THE BABY SWAP MIRACLE
MOTHER OF THE BRIDE

CHAPTER ONE

'ARE you OK?'

Was she?

She wasn't sure. Her heart was pounding, her legs felt like jelly and her stomach was rebelling, but it was Daisy's wedding day, so Amy dug around and dredged up some kind of a smile.

'I'm fine.'

'Sure?'

'Absolutely!' she lied, and tried to make the smile look more convincing. She didn't even need to ask how Daisy was. She was lit up from inside with a serene joy that was radiantly, blindingly obvious. Amy's smile wavered. She'd felt like that once, lifetimes ago.

She tweaked Daisy's dress for something to do and stood back. 'Are you ready?'

Her smile glowed brighter still. 'Oh, yes,' Daisy said softly. 'Do I look OK?'

Amy laughed indulgently and hugged her. 'You look stunning. Ben will be blown away.'

'I hope not, I want him here!' Daisy glanced down at Florence, fizzing silently on the end of Amy's arm, on her very best behaviour. She looked like a fairy in her pretty little dress and she was so excited Amy thought she was going to pop.

'OK, darling?' Daisy asked.

Florence nodded, her eyes like saucers, and for a second she looked so like Ben—so like Matt—that Amy's heart squeezed painfully with the ache of loss.

'Let's go then,' Daisy said, stooping to kiss her about-to-be stepdaughter, and with a quick, supportive hug for Amy that nearly unravelled her, she turned and took her father's arm.

As they gave the signal for the processional music, Amy sucked in a deep, slow breath.

You can do this, she told herself desperately. *Ignore him. Just keep your eyes on Daisy's back, and you'll be fine.*

And then with Florence at her side, she fell in behind them, her eyes glued on Daisy as they walked slowly down between the rows of guests to where Ben was waiting.

Ben, and Matt.

Don't look...

Matt's hair was slightly longer than his twin's, more tousled, the dark, silky strands so familiar that her fingers still remembered the feel of them. His back was ramrod straight, his shoulders broad, square, uncompromising.

She shouldn't have looked. She should have kept her eyes on Daisy, but they wouldn't obey her and her heart was pounding so hard she was sure he'd hear it.

Please don't turn round...

He didn't move a muscle.

He couldn't see her, but he could feel her there, getting closer. She was behind him, over his left shoulder, and there was no way he was turning round to look. Just getting through the ceremony was going to be hard enough, without making it harder by rubbing salt into the wound her presence here had ripped wide open.

Not that it had ever really healed.

Ben's hand brushed his, their fingers tangling and gripping for a second in a quick, wordless exchange.

You OK?

Sure. You?

Never better, and you're lying, but thanks for being here.

You're welcome. Wouldn't have it any other way.

Out of the corner of his eye Matt saw Daisy draw level with Ben, saw him reach out to her. He could feel their love like a halo around them, the huge depth of caring and emotion threatening to swamp him. The sort of love he'd felt for Amy...

Hang on in there. You can do it. It won't take long.

He heard Ben murmur something to Daisy, heard her murmur back, but he had no idea what they said. All his senses were trained on the woman standing behind Daisy. He could hear the rustle of her dress, feel the tension radiating off her, smell the slight drift of her achingly familiar perfume.

How could he be so aware of her? He closed his eyes, taking a moment to calm his thoughts, to settle it all down, to get the lid back on the box. There. He was fine. He could do this.

The ceremony began, and then it was his turn. All he had to do was to take the rings from his pocket and hand them over. Which meant he had to move, to turn—not far, but just far enough to see—

Amy...

The lid blew off the box with the force of an explosion, and he dropped the rings in Ben's outstretched hand and stepped sharply back to his place, his emotions reeling.

He had to concentrate on Ben and Daisy. This was their day, and he and Amy were in the past. Gone.

But not, apparently, forgotten.

Not by a long way.

The ceremony was interminable.

Her whole body was shaking and she was finding it really hard to concentrate on anything but Matt. Crazy, since she worked with Ben almost every day and they were scarily alike. The most identical of identical twins, with one huge difference—she loved Matt with all her broken, guarded heart, and today was the first time she'd had to face him in four years—

Don't go there!

She felt Florence wriggle at the end of her arm, and glanced down.

'You's squeezing me!' she whispered, and she realised she had a death grip on the little girl's hand. 'Sorry,' she mouthed, wincing, but Florence smiled up at her and patted her hand.

''S OK, Amy, I know you's scared,' she replied in a stage whisper that made several of the guests smile, and in the row beside her Amy heard Florence's mother give a quiet, despairing chuckle.

But then the ceremony was over, and Ben was kissing Daisy while everyone clapped and cheered, and Florence wriggled out of Amy's loosened grip and ran to them. Laughing, Ben scooped her up and kissed her, too, and as Amy watched Matt turned slowly towards her and their eyes met and locked.

Time stopped. She felt the room start to swim, and she dragged in a quick breath, then another. Matt frowned, then moved swiftly, his fingers gripping her elbow. 'Are you all right?' he murmured, his voice low, gruff and painfully familiar.

She swayed against him. All right? Not in a million years, but she wasn't telling him that. She straightened up.

'I'm fine. Low blood sugar,' she lied, and with a slight frown he let her go. Not that it made any difference. The skin of her arm was tingling from the touch of his fingers, her highly sensitised flesh branded by each one.

'We have to sign the register,' he said, and she nodded. They did. They should have done it years ago, but not like this. Not as witnesses...

'OK now?'

'Fine,' she said shortly, and took that vital and symbolic step away from him before she gave into the urge to turn her face into his chest and howl.

He thought it would never end.

The smiling, the greeting of old friends and family, the meeting of new people. And of course there were people there who'd known Amy. People who should have been at their wedding.

'Isn't that...?'

'Yes—small world, isn't it? She and Daisy are old friends. How are you? It's good to see you again...'

And on, and on, until he was ready to scream.

He drank rather more than was sensible, considering he had to make a speech, but every time he caught sight

of Amy it was as if he'd been drenched in iced water
and he felt stone cold sober. They sat down to eat at last,
strung out in a line with Ben and Daisy and two sets of
parents between them, and he was glad that his brother
and his new sister-in-law had opted for a long top table
instead of a round one.

Or maybe that was why they had, thinking ahead to
this moment.

Florence was with Jane and Peter at another table, and
he winked at her and she winked back, her little face
screwing up as she tried to shut just one eye. It made
him laugh, in an odd, detached way.

And then finally the food was eaten, the champagne
glasses were filled and it was time for the speeches.

Amy didn't want to listen to his speech, but she had little choice. None, in fact, but she loved Daisy and she'd
grown increasingly fond of Ben, and this was their wedding and she wanted to be here for it. And Matt wasn't
going to spoil it for her, she told herself firmly as Daisy's
father got to his feet.

He welcomed Ben to their family with a warmth in
his voice that made Daisy cry, then Ben gave a funny,
tender and rather endearing speech about Daisy and
the change she'd made to his life, thanked everyone for
coming to share their day, and then with a grin at Matt
he said, 'Now, before I hand you over to my clone for
the ritual character assassination I'm sure I've got coming, I'd like you to raise your glasses to two very special
and beautiful women. One is my wife's dearest friend,
Amy, and the other is my precious daughter, Florence. I
know Daisy's appreciated their support and their help in
giving us such a wonderful day to enjoy together. Amy

particularly has worked absolutely tirelessly on the arrangements, and I think she's done a brilliant job. And Florence has painstakingly decorated and filled the little favour boxes for you all, so we hope you enjoy them. Ladies and gentlemen, the bridesmaids!'

She was grateful to little Florence, who was kneeling up on her chair giggling and attracting all the eyes in the room, because it meant fewer people were looking at her while she struggled with her prickling eyes and the rising tide of colour on her cheeks.

And then it was Matt's turn, and he was smiling engagingly at everyone as if he did this kind of thing all the time. He probably did, she thought. He'd always had a way with words.

'You'll have to forgive my deluded brother,' he began drily. 'Being the firstborn just makes him the prototype, and we all know they need refining, but I'm very pleased to be here today because after thirty-four years of arguments, black eyes, mind-blowingly foolish stunts and some underhanded, downright cheating, it's been settled. I am officially the best man, and now we can move on with our lives!'

There was a ripple of laughter round the room, but then he went on, 'On the subject of twins, we didn't get to bed very early last night. Ben, Daisy and I ended up delivering two rather special babies shortly before midnight, and I found myself wondering, will those little girls have as much fun growing up as we did? Because it wasn't all fights. I always had a friend, a playmate, someone to lean on. Someone to swap with. We did that quite a lot—in fact, Daisy, are you sure that's Ben? You wouldn't be the first person to fall for it. I think Jenny Wainwright's still confused.'

'No, I'm quite sure, he's much more good-looking!' Daisy said, laughing and hugging Ben.

It sounded silly, but Amy absolutely understood how she felt. The similarities were obvious. The differences were more subtle but they were definitely there, not only in their looks but in their characters, and her reaction to them was utterly different.

Ben could talk to her and she just heard his words. Matt talked, and her soul seemed to tune into his—but right now, she didn't need that spiritual connection that seemed to call to every cell in her body. She didn't need to feel the rich tones of his deep, warm voice swirling round her, that slight Yorkshire accent teasing at her senses, and with an effort she made herself listen to what he was saying.

She was glad she did. He was very, very funny, but also very moving. He told tales of their childhood esca- pades, but also their closeness, their enduring friendship, and finally he wound up, and she felt her heart hammer because she knew—she just knew—he was going to look at her and she was going to have to smile.

'Now, my job—as the best man,' he added with a grin, 'is to thank Ben for his kind remarks about Daisy's beautiful bridesmaids, and I have to say he's right, Florence is the cutest little bridesmaid I've ever seen. And as for Amy…' He turned to face her, as she'd known he would, and his smile twisted a little. 'Well, it's my duty and privilege to escort this beautiful woman for the rest of the day, so sorry, guys, you'll have to find someone else to dance with. She's all mine. There have to be some perks to the job.'

Amy tried to smile as he tilted his glass to her,

drained it and sat down to cheers and applause, but it was a feeble attempt.

She was dreading the rest of the party. She would *have* to dance with him, and there was no getting out of it. As chief bridesmaid and best man, that was their role, but the irony wasn't lost on her.

As far as she was concerned, Matt wasn't the best man—he was the only man.

And when the chips were down, when she'd needed him most, he'd walked away.

'Good wedding—the hotel have looked after you well. It's a great venue.'

Ben smiled. 'Isn't it? We were really lucky to get it at such short notice. Good speech, by the way. Thank you.'

Matt frowned slightly, feeling another stab of guilt. 'Don't thank me. I wasn't there for you last time. I should have been.'

'No. You were absolutely right at the time, neither of us should have been there. I shouldn't have married Jane, and you weren't exactly in the right place to worry about me. You had enough going on with Amy. Matt, are you really OK with this?'

Matt met Ben's eyes briefly and looked away. 'Yeah, I'm fine.'

'Amy's not.'

'I know.'

'She still loves you.'

He snorted rudely and drained his glass. 'Hardly. I think she's finding it a little awkward, that's all. She'll be fine.'

Or she would as long as he kept avoiding her.

Ben made a soft, disbelieving noise and caught Daisy's eye. He nodded and looked back at Matt, his eyes seeing far too much for comfort. 'We're going to cut the cake now, and then have the first dance. And then—'

'I know.' He pretended to straighten Ben's cravat. 'Don't worry, I won't renege on my duties.'

'I wasn't suggesting you would. I was just going to say be kind to Amy.'

He looked up at Ben again, his older brother by mere moments, and laughed. 'What—like she was kind to me?'

'She was hurting.'

'And I wasn't?' He gave a harsh sigh and rammed a hand through his hair. 'Don't worry. I'll be good. You go and cut your cake and have your dance, and I'll play my part. I won't let you down.'

'It's not me I'm worried about,' Ben muttered, but Matt pushed him towards his wife and turned away. He didn't need to scan the room for Amy. His radar hadn't let him down. She was right there, by the French doors out onto the terrace, talking to two women that he didn't recognise.

One was visibly pregnant, the other had a baby in her arms, and for a moment his heart squeezed with pain. *Ahh, Amy...*

She could feel him watching her, the little hairs on the back of her neck standing to attention.

He was getting closer, she knew it. She'd managed to avoid him up to now, and she'd known it was too good to last.

'Excuse me, Amy—they're going to cut the cake and then have the first dance.'

And then it would be time for the second dance, the one she'd been dreading, and she'd have to dance with him and look—well, civilised would be a good thing to try for, she thought as she turned round to face him.

'OK. I'll come over. Give me a moment.'

She turned back to Katie and Laura, and after a second she felt him move away, and her shoulders sagged a fraction.

'Amy, are you all right, honey?' Katie asked, juggling the baby with one arm so she could hug her.

She returned the hug briefly and straightened up, easing away. 'I'm fine.'

'Well, you don't look fine,' Laura said, her eyes narrowing. 'Are you sick? You're awfully pale.'

'I'm just tired. It's been a busy week. I'd better go.'

She left them, letting out a soft sigh as she walked away. She'd never told them about Matt, and she'd asked Daisy not to discuss it. The fewer people at the wedding who knew they had history, the better. It was hard enough facing his mother, who'd given her a swift, gentle hug and patted her back as if she was soothing a child.

She'd nearly cried. She'd loved Liz. She'd been endlessly kind to her, incredibly welcoming, and she hadn't seen her since—

'Amy, we're going to— Gosh, sweetheart, are you all right?'

Daisy's face was puckered with concern, and Amy rolled her eyes.

'Daisy, don't fuss, I'm just tired. We didn't go to bed

till nearly one and the cat was walking all over me all night. And we've been up for hours, if you remember.'

'I know. I just—'

'I'm fine,' she said firmly. 'Matt said you're going to cut the cake.'

'We are. Amy, are you sure you can do this? If you want to leave—'

'I don't want to leave! It's your wedding! Go and cut the cake, and we can have champagne and cake and dancing and it'll be wonderful. Now shoo.'

Amy turned her round and pushed her towards her husband, who held his hand out to her and drew her into his arms for yet another kiss.

'They do seem genuinely happy together.'

She froze. How had he crept up on her? She hadn't felt him approaching—maybe because she'd been so intensely aware of him all day that her senses were overloaded.

'They are,' she said, her voice a little ragged. 'They're wonderful together.'

'She's very fond of you.'

'It's mutual. She's lovely. She's been through a lot, and she's been a really good friend to me.'

'Which is why you're here, when you'd rather be almost anywhere else in the world.'

'Speak for yourself.'

He gave a soft huff of laughter, teasing the hair on the back of her neck. 'I was,' he answered, and despite the laugh, his voice had a hollow ring to it. 'Still, needs must. Right, here we go. I think Ben's going to make a bit of a speech to welcome the evening guests before they cut the cake.'

He was still standing behind her, slightly to one side,

and she could feel his breath against her bare shoulder, feel the warmth radiating from his big, solid body.

The temptation to lean back into him—to rest her head against his cheek, to feel him curve his hand round her hip and ease her closer as he would have done before—nearly overwhelmed her. Instead, she stepped away slightly, pretending to shift so she could see them better, but in fact she could see perfectly well, and he must have realised that.

She heard him sigh, and for some crazy reason it made her feel sad. Crazy, because it had been him that had left her, walking away just when she needed him the most, so why on earth should she feel sad for him? So he was still alone, according to Ben. So what? So was she. There were worse things than being alone. At least it was safe.

'Daisy chose the music for our first dance,' Ben was saying, his smile wry. 'It has a special meaning for us. While we're dancing, I'd like you to imagine the moment we met—just about thirty seconds after the kitchen ceiling and half a bath of water came down on my head.'

And with that, they cut the cake, the lights were dimmed and the band started playing 'The First Time Ever I Saw Your Face'.

There was a ripple of laughter and applause, but then they all went quiet as Ben, still smiling, drew Daisy into his arms as if she was the most precious thing he'd ever held.

Damn, Amy thought, sniffing hard, and then a tissue arrived in her hand, on a drift of cologne that brought back so many memories she felt the tears well even faster.

'OK?'

No, she wasn't. She was far from OK, she thought crossly, and she wished everyone would stop asking her that.

'I'm fine.'

He sighed softly. 'Look, Amy, I know this is awkward, but we just have to get through it for their sakes. I don't want to do it any more than you do, but it's not for long.'

Long enough. A second in his arms would be long enough to tear her heart wide open—

The dance was over, the music moved on and without hesitation Matt took her hand, the one with the tissue still clutched firmly in it, led her onto the dance floor and turned her into his arms.

'Just pretend you don't hate me,' he told her, with a smile that didn't reach his eyes, and she breathed in, needing oxygen, and found nothing but that cologne again.

Holding her was torture.

A duty and a privilege, as he'd said in his speech?

Or just an agonising reminder of all he'd lost?

She had one hand on his shoulder, the other cradled in his left, and his right hand was resting lightly against her waist, so he could feel the slender column of her spine beneath his splayed fingers, the shift of her ribs as she breathed, the flex of the muscles as she moved in time to the music. She felt thinner, he thought. Well, she would. The last time he'd held her, he thought with a wave of sadness, she'd been pregnant with their child.

One dance merged into another, and then another. He eased her closer, and with a sigh that seemed to shudder through her body, she rested her head on his shoulder and yielded to the gentle pressure of his hand. Her thighs brushed his, and he felt heat flicker along his veins. Oh, Amy. He'd never forgotten her, never moved on. Not really.

And as he cradled her against his chest, her pale gold hair soft under his cheek, he realised he'd been treading water for years, just waiting for the moment when he could hold her again.

He sighed, and she felt his warm breath tease her hair, sending tiny shivers running through her like fairies dancing over her skin. It made her feel light-headed again, and she stepped back.

'I need some air,' she mumbled, and tried to walk away, but her hand was still firmly wrapped in his, and he followed her, ushering her through the crowd and out of the French doors into the softly lit courtyard. Groups of people were standing around talking quietly, laughing, and she breathed in the cooler air with a sigh of relief.

'Better?'

She nodded. 'Yes. Thanks.'

'Don't thank me. You look white as a sheet. Have you eaten today?'

'We just had a meal.'

'And you hardly touched it. My guess is you didn't have lunch, either, and you probably skipped breakfast. No wonder you had low blood sugar earlier. Come on, let's go and raid the buffet. I didn't eat much, either, and I'm starving.'

He was right on all counts. She *was* hungry, and she *had* skipped lunch, but only because she'd lost her breakfast. She never could eat when she was nervous, and she'd been so, so nervous for the last few days her stomach had been in knots, and this morning it had rebelled. And that dizzy spell could well have been low blood sugar, now she came to think about it.

'It's probably not a bad idea,' she conceded, and let him lead her to the buffet table. She put a little spoonful of something on her plate, and he growled, shoved his plate in her other hand and loaded them both up.

'I can't eat all that!' she protested, but he speared her with a look from those implacable blue eyes and she gave up. He could put it on the plate. Didn't mean she had to eat it.

'I'll help you. Come on, let's find a quiet corner.'

He scooped up two sets of cutlery, put them in his top pocket, snagged a couple of glasses of wine off a passing waiter and shepherded her across the floor and back out to the courtyard.

'OK out here, or is it too cold for you in that dress?'

'It's lovely. It's a bit warm in there.'

'Right. Here, look, there's a bench.'

He steered her towards it, handed her a glass and sat back, one ankle on the other knee and the plate balanced on his hand while he attacked the food with his fork.

He'd always eaten like that, but that was medicine for you, eating on the run. Maybe he thought they should get it over with and then he could slide off and drink with the boys. Well, if the truth be told he didn't have to hang around for her.

'You're not eating.'

'I'm too busy wondering why you don't have chronic indigestion, the speed you're shovelling that down.'

He gave a short chuckle. 'Sorry. Force of habit. And I was starving.' He put the plate down for a moment and picked up his glass. 'So, how are you, really?'

Really? She hesitated, the fork halfway to her mouth. Did he honestly want to know? Probably not.

'I'm fine.'

'How's the job?'

'OK. I like it. As with any job it has its ups and downs. Mostly ups. The hospital's a good place to work.'

'Yes, so Ben says.' He stared pensively down into his glass, swirling it slowly. 'You didn't have to leave London, you know. We were never going to bump into each other at different hospitals.'

No? She wasn't sure—not sure enough, at least, that she'd felt comfortable staying there. Up here, she'd been able to relax—until Ben had arrived. Ever since then she'd been waiting for Matt to turn up unexpectedly on the ward to visit his brother, and the monoamniotic twins they'd delivered last night had been something he'd taken a special interest in, so once Melanie Grieves had been admitted, she'd been on tenterhooks all the time. Waiting for the other shoe to drop.

Well, now it had, and it was every bit as bad as she'd expected.

'I like it here, it was a good move for me,' she said, and then changed the subject firmly. 'Who's Jenny Wainwright?'

He laughed, a soft, warm chuckle that told her a funny story was coming. 'Ben's first girlfriend. We were thirteen or so. They'd been dating for weeks, and she wouldn't let him kiss her, so I talked him into letting me take his place on the next date, to see if I had more luck.'

'And did you?'

His mouth twisted into a wry smile. 'No. Not that time. I did about two years later, though, at a party, and she told me he kissed better, so I went and practised on someone else.'

She laughed, as he'd wanted her to, but all she could think was that whoever he'd practised on had taught him well. She ought to thank her—except of course he wasn't hers to kiss any more. Regret swamped her, and as she looked across and met his eyes, she saw tenderness in them and a gentle, puzzled sadness. 'I've missed you,' he said softly, and she gulped down a sudden, convulsive little sob.

'I've missed you, too,' she admitted, her voice unsteady.

He stared at her searchingly, then glanced down. 'Are you all done with that food?'

Food? She looked at her plate. She'd eaten far more than she'd thought she would, to her surprise, and she was feeling much better. 'Yes. Do you want the rest?'

'No, I'm fine, but I'm supposed to be entertaining you, so let's go and dance.'

Out of duty? Or because he wanted to? She hesitated for a second, then stood up, raising an eyebrow at him. Whichever, she wanted to dance with him, and she wasn't going to get another chance.

'Come on, then, if you really want to.'

Oh, yes. He wanted. He got to his feet and led her back to the dance floor.

She'd always loved dancing, and he loved dancing with her, loved the feel of her body, the lithe, supple limbs, the sleek curves, the warmth of her against him.

He didn't get to hold her, though, not at first. The tempo was fast—too fast, he decided, after a couple of dances, so he reeled her in and halved the beat, cherishing the moment because he knew it wouldn't last. How could it, with all they had behind them? But now—he had her now, in his arms, against his heart, and his body ached for her.

The tempo slowed, moving seamlessly from one un-ashamedly romantic, seductive number to another, until they were swaying against each other, her arms draped around his neck, his hands splayed against her back, the fingers of one hand resting lightly on the warm, soft skin above the back of her dress, the other hand lower, so all he had to do was slip it down a fraction and he could cup the firm swell of her bottom and ease her closer...

She felt his hand move, felt him draw her in so she could feel every move he made. Their legs had somehow meshed together so his thigh was between hers, nudging gently with every slight shift of his body, brushing the soft silk of her dress against her legs and driving out all her common sense.

She knew him so well, had danced with him so many times, and it was so easy to rest against him, to lay her head against his chest and listen to the deep, steady thud of his heart, to slide her fingers through his hair and sift the silky strands that she remembered so well.

Easier, still, to turn her head, to feel the graze of stubble against her temple and tilt her face towards him, to feel the soft warmth of his lips as they took hers in a tentative, questioning kiss.

I love you...

Had he said that? Had she?

She lifted her head and touched her lips to his again, and his breath seared over her skin in a shuddering sigh.

'Amy—'

'Matt...'

He lifted his head and stared down at her in the dim light on the edge of the dance floor, their eyes locked as each of them battled against the need raging within them. She could feel him fighting it, feel herself losing just as he closed his eyes and unclasped her hands from behind his neck, sliding his hand down her arm and linking their fingers as he led her off the dance floor and up the broad, sweeping staircase to the floor above in a tense, brittle silence.

They didn't speak to anyone. They passed people in the hall, people on the stairs—they didn't stop, didn't look left or right, until the door of his room was opened and closed again behind them, and then he cradled her face and stared down into her eyes once more.

Still he didn't speak, and neither did she. What was there to say? Nothing that would make any sense.

Slowly, with infinite tenderness, he touched his lips to hers again, and she whimpered softly and clutched at him, desperate for the feel of him, for his body on her, in her, surrounding and filling her.

'Please,' she whispered silently, but he heard her and took a step back, stripping without finesse, heeling off his beautiful handmade shoes, his hired suit hitting the floor and crumpling in a heap. After a brief fight with his cufflinks the shirt followed, then the boxers, the socks, and he spun her and searched blindly for the zip.

'Here.' She lifted her arm so he could find it, sucking her breath in as he tugged it down and the dress fell to the floor, puddling round her ankles and leaving her standing there in nothing but a tiny scrap of lace.

A rough groan was torn from his throat and he lifted her in his arms and lowered her carefully to the middle of the bed. Fingers shaking, he hooked his fingers into the lace at her hips, easing it away, following its path down the length of her legs with his lips, the slight roughness of his stubble grazing the sensitive skin as he inched his way to her feet, driving her to the edge.

He turned his head, looked back at her, and his eyes were black with need. She whimpered, her legs twitching under his warm, firm hands, and he moved, nudging her thighs apart, so nearly there—and then he froze, his face agonised.

'Amy, we can't—I haven't—'

'I'm on the Pill.'

The breath sighed out of him in a rush, and he gathered her into his arms, held her for a moment, and then his lips found hers again and he was there, filling her, bringing a sob of relief from her as his body slid home and she tightened around him.

'Matt...'

'Oh, God, Amy, I've missed you,' he whispered, and then he started to move, his body shaking with control until she was sick of waiting and arched under him, her hands tugging at him, begging for more.

And he gave her more, pulling out all the stops, driving her higher and higher until she came apart in his arms, her reserve splintering under the onslaught of his unleashed passion.

Then he held her, his body shuddering in release, his heart slamming against his ribs so hard he thought they'd break, until gradually it slowed and he rolled to his side, taking her with him, their bodies still locked together as the aftershocks of their lovemaking faded slowly away into the night.

CHAPTER TWO

HE MADE love to her again in the night, reaching for her in the darkness, bringing her body slowly awake with sure, gentle hands and whispered kisses. She laid her hand tenderly against his cheek, savouring the rasp of stubble against her palm, her thumb dragging softly over the firm fullness of his lower lip.

He opened his mouth, drawing her thumb inside and sucking it deeply, his tongue exploring it, his teeth nipping lightly and making the breath catch in her throat. She shifted so she could reach him, her hands running over him now, checking for changes and finding only sweet, familiar memories. He moved on, his mouth warm and moist against her skin, and she joined in, their lips tracing tender trails across each other's bodies. They were taking their time now for leisurely explorations, the darkness shielding them from emotions they couldn't bear to expose—emotions too dark, too painful to consider.

That wasn't what this night was about, Amy thought later as she lay awake beside him listening to the deep, even rhythm of his breathing. It was for old times' sake, no-longer lovers reaching out to touch fleetingly what had once been theirs to love.

She was under no illusions. After the wedding, Matt would be going back to London, and she'd be staying here, nursing her still-broken heart but with a little more tenderness, a little more forgiveness in her soul. He wasn't indifferent. Clearly not. But their lives had moved on, gone in different directions, and maybe it was for the best.

Maybe this was the way forward, for both of them. A little healing salve smeared gently over their wounds, kissing each other better.

She shifted slightly, seeking the warmth of his body, and he reached for her again in his sleep, drawing her closer, their legs tangled, her head pillowed on his shoulder as she slept, until the first light of dawn crept round the edges of the curtains.

He woke her gently, his voice a soft murmur in her ear.

'Amy?'

'Mmm.'

'Amy, it's morning.'

'Mmm.'

'You're in my room.'

'Mmm. I know.'

'Sweetheart, *everyone* will know soon.'

Her eyes flew open, and she sucked in a breath, the night coming back to her in a flood of memory and sudden awkwardness. 'Oh, rats. Damn. Um—Matt, help me get dressed.'

She threw the quilt off and starting searching for her underwear. Stupid, stupid… 'Where the hell are my pants?'

Pants? He nearly laughed. Try cobwebs.

'Take the dressing gown on the back of the door—have you got your room key?'

'Yes, of course. It's—'

In her clutch bag, which was—somewhere. She flopped back down onto the edge of the bed, dragging the quilt back over herself to hide her body from his eyes. Pointless, after he'd explored it so thoroughly, knew it so well in any case, but she was suddenly smitten with shyness. 'It's in my clutch bag,' she admitted.

'Which is…?'

Good question. 'Downstairs?'

He groaned and rolled away from her, vanishing into the bathroom and emerging a few minutes later damp, tousled and unshaven. And stark naked, the water drops still clinging to his body gleaming in the spill of light from the bathroom door and drawing her hungry eyes. He flipped open his overnight bag, pulled out some jeans and boxers and a shirt, dressed quickly and took the room key out of the door lock.

'What's your bag look like?' he asked briskly, and she dragged her mind off his body and tried to concentrate.

'Cream satin, about so big, little bronzy chain. It's got a lipstick, a tissue and the room key in it.'

'Any ideas where?'

She shrugged. 'The edge of the dance floor? I put it down at one point.'

He left her there, hugging her knees in the middle of the bed, looking rumpled and gorgeous and filled with regret.

He knew all about that one. How could he have been so stupid?

And why was she on the Pill, for heaven's sake? Was

she in a relationship? Or did she do this kind of thing all the time?

Hell, he hoped not. The thought of his Amy casually—

He swallowed hard and ran downstairs, to find that staff were already starting the mammoth clean-up operation.

'I'm looking for a cream satin evening bag,' he told someone, and was directed to the night porter's office.

'This the one?'

He wasn't sure, so he opened it and found exactly what she'd said inside. Well, if the room key fitted...

He went to it, and it gave him immediate access. Her case was there, unopened, inside the unused room, and he carried it back to her.

'Oh, Matt, you're a star. Thank you.'

'Anything to spare a lady's blushes. I'll go to your room,' he said, 'and if anyone knocks on the door, just ignore them. It'll only be Ben or my parents, and they'll ring me if it's anything important.'

He slipped his mobile into his pocket, picked up his wallet and did the same, then gave Amy an awkward smile. 'I guess I'll see you at breakfast.'

She nodded, looking embarrassed now, her grey eyes clouded with something that could have been shame, and without dragging it out he left her there and went to the room that should have been hers, lay on the bed and let his breath out on a long, ragged sigh.

What a fool. All he'd done, all he'd proved, was that he'd never stopped loving her. Well, hell, he'd known that before. It had hardly needed underlining.

He rolled to his side, thumped the pillow into the side of his neck and tried to sleep.

* * *

How could she have been so stupid?

She'd known seeing him again would be dangerous to her, but she hadn't realised how dangerous. She pulled the hotel gown tighter round her waist and moved to the chair by the window. She had a view over the courtyard where they'd had their buffet supper, could see the bench if she craned her neck.

Sudden unexpected tears glazed her eyes, and she swiped them away and sniffed hard. She'd done some stupid things in her life, most of them with Matt, and this was just the icing on the cake.

She got up and put the little kettle on to make tea, and found her pills in her washbag and popped one out. Thank God for synthetic hormones, she thought drily as she swallowed the pill. Or maybe not, because without the medication to control her irregular periods, they would never have spent the night together.

Which would have been a *good* thing, she told herself firmly. But telling him she was on the Pill was a two-edged sword. He probably thought she was a slut.

'I don't care what he thinks, it's none of his damn business and at least I won't get pregnant again,' she said to the kettle, and made herself a cup of tea and sat cradling it and staring down into the courtyard until it was stone cold.

And then she nearly dropped it, because Matt was there, outside in the courtyard garden just below her, sitting on the bench with a cup in his hand and checking something on his phone.

He made a call, then put the cup down and walked swiftly across the courtyard out of sight. One of his patients in London needing his attention? Or Melanie

Grieves, mother of the little twins they'd delivered on Friday night?

Or just coming inside to see whoever he'd spoken to—his parents, maybe?

Moments later, there was a soft knock at the door.

'Amy? It's Matt.'

She let him in reluctantly and tried to look normal and less like an awkward teenager. 'Everything OK?'

'Yes. I'm going to see Melanie Grieves. Ben asked me to keep an eye on her.'

She nodded. 'Are you coming back for breakfast and to say goodbye to everyone?'

'Yes. I don't want to be lynched. Let me take my stuff, and I'll get out of your way. Here's your room key. Hang onto mine as well for now. I'll get it off you later.' He scooped up the suit, the shirt, the underwear, throwing them in the bag any old how and zipping it, and then he hesitated. For a second she thought he was about to kiss her, but then he just picked up his bag and left without a backward glance.

Amy let out the breath she'd been holding since he'd come in, and sat down on the end of the bed. There was no point in hanging around in his room, she thought. She'd shower and dress, and go downstairs and see if anyone was around.

Unlikely. The party had gone on long after they'd left it, and everyone was probably still in bed—where she would be, in her own room, if she had a grain of sense.

Well, she'd proved beyond any reasonable doubt that she didn't, she thought, and felt the tears welling again.

Damn him. Damn him for being so—so—just so *irresistible*. Well, never again. Without his body beside her, without the feel of his warmth, the tenderness of his touch, it all seemed like a thoroughly bad idea, and she knew the aftermath of it would haunt her for ages.

Years.

Forever?

Melanie Grieves was fine.

Her wound was healing, her little twins were doing very well and apart from a bit of pain she was over the moon. He hadn't really needed to come and see her, he'd just had enough of sitting around in the hotel beating himself up about Amy.

Not that he shouldn't be doing that. He'd been a total idiot, and she really, really didn't need him falling all over her like he had last night. And leaving the dance floor like that—God knows what everyone had thought of them. He hadn't even asked her, just dragged her up the stairs and into his room like some kind of caveman.

He growled in frustration and slammed the car door shut. He'd better go back, better show his face and try and lie his way out of it. Better still, find Amy and get their story straight before his mother got her side of it and bent his ear. She'd always taken Amy's side.

Oh, hell.

He dropped his head forwards and knocked it gently against the hard, leatherbound steering wheel. Such a fool. And his head hurt. Good. It would remind him not to drink so much in future. He'd thought he was sober enough, but obviously not. If he'd been sober—

His phone rang and he pulled it out of his pocket and stared at the screen. Ben. Damn.

He ignored it. He'd talk to Amy first—if he got to her before they did. If only he had her number. She'd probably changed it, but maybe not. He dialled it anyway as he turned into the hotel car park, and she answered on the second ring.

'Hello?'

'Amy, it's Matt. We need to talk—we will have been seen last night. Where are you now?'

'Oh, damn. In the courtyard. Bring coffee.'

Stressed as he was, he smiled at that. He found a breakfast waitress and ordered a pot of coffee and a basket of bacon rolls, then went and found her.

She was waiting, her heart speeding up as she caught sight of him, her nerves on edge. She couldn't believe what she'd done, couldn't believe she was going to sit here with him and concoct some cock-and-bull story to tell his family. Her friends. Oh, lord…

'How's Mel?' she asked, sticking to something safe.

'Fine. The babies are both doing well.'

'Good. Ben and Daisy'll be pleased.'

Silence. Of course there was, she thought. What was there to say, for heaven's sake? *Thank you for the best sex I've had in over four years? Not to say the only…?*

'Any sign of the others?' he asked after the silence had stretched out into the hereafter, and she shook her head.

'No. I put my bag in the car. Here's your room key. So—what's the story?'

'We wanted to talk?'

'We didn't talk, Matt,' she reminded him bluntly.

Pity they hadn't, she thought for the thousandth time. If they'd talked, they might have had more sense.

'You were feeling sick?' he suggested.

'What—from all that champagne?'

'It's not impossible.'

'I had less than you.'

'I think it's probably fair to say we both had more than was sensible,' he said drily, and she had to agree, but not out loud. She wasn't feeling that magnanimous.

'Maybe nobody noticed?' she said without any real conviction, and he gave a short, disbelieving laugh.

'Dream on, Amy. I dragged you off the dance floor and up the stairs in full view of everyone. I think someone will have noticed.'

She groaned and put her face in her hands, and then he started to laugh again, a soft, despairing sound that made her lift her head and meet his eyes. 'What?'

'I have some vague recollection of passing my parents in the hall.'

She groaned again. It just got better and better.

'Maybe you thought I needed to lie down?' she suggested wildly. 'Perhaps I'd told you I was feeling rough? It's not so unlikely, and it's beginning to look like the best option.'

'We could always tell them the truth.'

If we knew what it was, she thought, but the waitress arrived then with the tray of coffee and bacon rolls, and she seized one and sank her teeth into it and groaned. 'Oh, good choice,' she mumbled, and he laughed.

'Our default hangover food,' he said, bringing the memories crashing back. 'Want some ketchup?'

'That's disgusting,' she said, watching him squirt a dollop into his bacon roll and then demolish it in three bites before reaching for another. The times they'd done that, woken up on the morning after the night before and he'd cooked her bacon rolls and made her coffee.

He'd done that after their first night together, she remembered. And when she'd come out of hospital after—

She put the roll down and reached for her coffee, her appetite evaporating.

'So when are you off?' she asked.

'Tuesday morning,' he said, surprising her. 'Things are quiet at work at the moment, so I said I'd keep an eye on Mel till Ben and Daisy get back. They're only away for two nights.'

'Are you staying here?'

'No. I'm going back to Ben's.'

She nodded. It made sense, but she wasn't thrilled. She'd be tripping over him in the hospital at random times, bumping into him at Daisy's house when she went to feed Tabitha—because if he was next door at Ben's, there was no way she was going to stay there, as she'd half thought she might, to keep the cat company.

Or moving in and renting it as they'd suggested, come to that. Not after last night's folly. The last thing she wanted was to be bumping into Ben's brother every time he came up to visit them.

Daisy had stayed in her own house adjoining Ben's until the wedding because of Florence, but she'd be moving into his half when they came back, and they'd offered her Daisy's house. They wanted a tenant they could trust, and her lease was coming up for renewal, and it was a lot nicer than her flat for all sorts of reasons.

It had off-road parking, a garden, a lovely conservatory—and the best neighbours in the world. She'd been debating whether to take it, because of the danger of bumping into Matt who was bound to be coming back and forth to visit them, but after this—well, how could she relax?

She couldn't. It would have been bad enough before.

'Why don't we just tell them to mind their own business?' she suggested at last. 'It really is nothing to do with them if we chose to—'

She broke off, and he raised a brow thoughtfully.

'Chose to—?'

But his phone rang, and he scanned the screen and answered it, pulling a face.

'Hi, Ben.'

'Is that a private party over there, or can we join you?'

He looked up, and saw his brother and brand-new sister-in-law standing in the doorway watching them across the courtyard.

Amy followed the direction of his eyes, and sighed.

'Stand by to be grilled like a kipper,' she muttered, and stood up to hug Daisy. 'Well, good morning. How's the head?'

Daisy smiled smugly, looking very pleased with herself. 'Clear as a bell. In case you didn't notice, I wasn't drinking.'

Amy frowned, then looked from one to the other and felt the bottom fall out of her stomach. Ben's eyes were shining, and there was a smile he couldn't quite hide. 'Oh—that's wonderful,' she said softly, and then to her utter humiliation her eyes welled over. She hugged Daisy hard, then turned to Ben—just in time to see Matt release him with a look in his eyes she hadn't seen since—

'Congratulations, that's amazing,' he said gruffly, and gathered Daisy up and hugged her, too, his expression carefully veiled now.

Except that Amy could still see it, lingering in the back of his eyes, a fleeting echo of a grief once so raw it had torn them apart.

'So, when's it due?' he asked, going through the motions. Not that he wasn't interested, but today of all days...

'The tenth of May. It's very, very early on,' Daisy said wryly. 'I did the test this morning.'

'Right after she threw up.'

Matt gave a soft huff of sympathetic laughter. 'Poor Daisy. It passes, I'm reliably informed by my patients.' *That's right, keep it impersonal...*

'It's a good sign,' Amy said, her voice slightly strained to his ears. 'Means the pregnancy's secure.'

Unlike hers. Oh, God, beam me up...

'Changing the subject, it's none of my business, but—' Ben began, but Matt knew exactly where this was going and cut him off.

'You're right, it's not. We needed to talk, there were a lot of people about. Amy slept in my room, and I went to hers.'

At a quarter to six this morning, but they didn't need to know that, and he was darned sure they wouldn't have been up and about that early. But someone was.

'Yeah, Mum said she saw you coming out of your room and going to another one at some ungodly hour.'

Damn. Of all the people...

'I went to get my phone so I could ring the hospital,' he lied, but he'd never been able to lie convincingly to Ben, and as their eyes met he saw Ben clock the lie and yet say nothing.

As he'd said himself, it was none of his business, and he obviously realised he'd overstepped the mark. He'd back him up, though, if their mother said any more, of that Matt was sure. 'So how is Mel?' Ben asked, moving smoothly on, and Matt let out a slight sigh of relief.

'Fine. They're all fine. I've been in to see them, and

they're all doing really well. She was keen to hear all about the wedding. I promised I'd take her some cake—unless you want to do it when you come back?'

'No, you go for it. I'm glad she's well. Thanks for going in.'

'My pleasure. Did you order coffee or do you want me to do it?'

Daisy pulled a face. 'Can we have something less smelly, and something to eat? I really don't think I can wait till breakfast.'

'Sure. I'll order decaf tea. What about bacon rolls?'

'Oh, yes-s-s-s!' she said fervently. 'Amazing! Matt, you're a genius.'

He smiled, glancing across at Amy and sensing, rather than seeing, the sadness that lingered in her. She was smiling at Daisy, but underneath it all was grief, no longer raw and untamed, maybe, but there for all that.

Would it ever get easier? Ever truly go away?

He hoped so, but he was very much afraid that he was wrong.

'Well, hello, Mummy Grieves! Are you up for visitors?'

'Oh, yes! Hello, Amy, how are you? How was the wedding? Did Daisy look beautiful?'

'Utterly gorgeous, but I bet she wasn't as gorgeous as your little girls. Aren't you going to introduce me?'

'Of course. I hope you don't mind, but we've called them Daisy and Amy, because you two have been so kind and we really love the names.'

'Oh, that's so sweet of you, thank you,' Amy said, her eyes filling. In a rare complication, the twins had shared the same amniotic sac, and the danger of their cords tangling had meant Mel had been monitored as an inpatient for several weeks, and she and Daisy had got to know Mel very well. And this... She blinked hard and sniffed, and Mel hugged her.

'Thank *you*,' she corrected. 'So, this is Amy. Want a cuddle?'

'I'd better not—infection risk,' she lied. That was why she'd gone on her way in, so her clothes were clean, but the last thing she wanted was to hold them. Delivering babies was one thing. Going out of her way to cuddle them—well, she just didn't.

She admired them both, though, Amy first, then Daisy, their perfect little features so very alike and yet slightly different. 'Can you tell them apart yet?' she asked Mel, and she smiled and nodded.

'Oh, yes. I could see the differences straight away. Adrian can't always, but he'll learn, I expect. And Mr Walker and his brother—they're very alike, too, aren't they, but I can tell the difference. There's just something.'

Amy swallowed. Oh, yes. Ben didn't have the ability to turn her into a total basket case just by walking into the room, and just to prove it, Matt strolled in then and she felt her stomach drop to the floor and her heart lurch.

'Talk of the Devil,' she said brightly, and saying goodbye to Mel, she slipped past him, trying not to breath in the faint, lingering scent of soap and cologne, but it drifted after her on the air.

Just one more day. He'll be gone tomorrow.

It couldn't come soon enough...

He found her, the next day, working in the ward office filling out patient records on the computer.

'I'm off,' he said, and she looked up and wondered why, when she'd been so keen to see him go, she should feel a pang of sadness that she was losing him.

Ridiculous. She wasn't losing him, he wasn't hers! And anyway, since the wedding they'd hardly seen each other. But that didn't mean they hadn't both been painfully, desperately aware. Yet he hadn't once, in all that time, suggested they repeat the folly of Saturday night—

'Got time for a coffee?'

She glanced up at the clock. Actually, she had plenty of time. There was nothing going on, for once, and although no doubt now she'd thought that all hell would break loose, for the minute, anyway, it was quiet.

Did she *want* to make time for a coffee? Totally different question.

'I can spare five minutes,' she said, logging off the computer and sliding back her chair.

He ushered her through the door first, his hand resting lightly on the small of her back, and she felt the warmth, the security of it all the way through to her bones. Except it was a false sense of security.

'We ought to talk,' he said quietly, once they were seated in the café.

She stirred her coffee, chasing the froth round the top, frowning at it as if it held the answers. 'Is there anything to say?'

He laughed, a short, harsh sound that cut the air. 'Amy, we spent the *night* together,' he said—unnecessarily, since she'd hardly forgotten.

'For old times' sake,' she pointed out. 'That was all.'

'Was it? Was it really?'

'Yes. It really was.'

He stared at her, searching her eyes for the longest moment, and then the expression in them was carefully banked and he looked away. 'OK. If that's what you want.'

It wasn't. She wanted *him*, but she couldn't trust him, because when her world had disintegrated and she'd needed him more than she'd ever needed anybody in her life, he'd turned his back on her.

She wasn't going through that again, not for him, not for anybody.

'It is what I want,' she lied. 'It didn't work, Matt, and there's no use harking back to it. We need to let it go.'

His eyes speared her. 'Have you?'

Let it go? *Let her baby go?*

She sucked in a breath and looked away.

'I didn't think so,' he said softly. 'Well, if it helps you any, neither have I. And I haven't forgotten you, Amy.'

She closed her eyes, wishing he would go, wishing he could stay. She heard the scrape of a chair, felt the touch of his hand on her shoulder.

'You know where I am if you change your mind.'

'I won't,' she vowed. She couldn't. She didn't dare. She simply wasn't strong enough to survive a second time.

He bent, tipped her head back with his fingers and dropped the gentlest, sweetest, saddest kiss on her lips.

'Goodbye, Amy. Take care of yourself.'

And then he was gone, walking swiftly away, leaving her there alone in the middle of the crowded café. She wanted to get up, to run after him, to yell at him to stop, she was sorry, she didn't mean it, please stay. But she didn't.

Somehow, just barely, she managed to stop herself, and no doubt one day she'd be grateful for that.

But right now, she felt as if she'd just thrown away her last chance at happiness, and all she wanted to do was cry.

CHAPTER THREE

IT TOOK her weeks to work out what was going on.

Weeks in which Matt was in her head morning, noon and night. She kept telling herself she'd done the right thing, that not seeing him again was sensible, but it wasn't easy to convince herself. Not easy at all, and Daisy and Ben being so blissfully happy didn't help.

She ached for him so much it was physical, but she'd done the right thing, sending him away. She had. She couldn't rely on him, couldn't trust him again with her heart. And she was genuinely relieved when her period came right on cue, because although she might want *him*, the thought of going through another pregnancy terrified her, and for the first time since the wedding she felt herself letting go of an inner tension she hadn't even been aware of.

She could move on now. They'd said their goodbyes, and it was done.

Finished.

The autumn came and went, and December arrived with a vengeance. It rained, and when it wasn't raining, it was sleeting, and then it dried up and didn't thaw for days. And her boiler broke down in her flat.

Marvellous, she thought. Just what she needed. She contacted her landlord, but it would be three weeks before it could be replaced—more, maybe, because plumbers were rushed off their feet after the freeze— and so she gave in to Ben and Daisy's gentle nagging, and moved into Daisy's house just ten days before Christmas.

'It's only temporary, till my boiler's fixed,' she told them firmly, but they just smiled and nodded and refused to take any rent on the grounds that it was better for the house to be occupied.

Then Daisy had her twenty-week scan, and of course she asked to see the photo. What else could she do? And she thought she'd be fine, she saw them all the time in her work, but it really got to her. Because of the link to Matt? She had no idea, but it haunted her that day and the next, popping up in every quiet moment and bringing with it a rush of grief that threatened to undermine her. She and Matt had been so happy, so deliriously overjoyed back then. And then, so shortly before her scan was due—

A laugh jerked her out of her thoughts, a laugh so like Matt's that it could so easily have been him, and she felt her heart squeeze. Stupid. She *knew* it was Ben. She heard him laugh all the time. And every time, she felt pain like a solid ball wedged in her chest.

She *missed* him. So, so much.

'Oh, Amy, great, I was hoping I'd find you here. New admission—thirty-four weeks, slight show last night, mild contractions which could just be Braxton Hicks'. Have you got time to admit her for me, please? She's just moved to the area last week, so we haven't seen her before but she's got her hand-held notes.'

She swiped the tears from her cheeks surreptitiously while she pretended to stifle a yawn. 'Sure. I could do with a break from this tedious admin. I'll just log off and I'll be with you. What's her name?'

'Helen Kendall. She's in the assessment room.'

Amy found her sitting on the edge of the chair looking worried and guilty, and she introduced herself.

'I'm so sorry to just come in,' Helen said, 'but I was worried because I've been really overdoing it with the move and I'm just so *tired*,' she blurted out, and then she started to cry.

'Oh, Helen,' Amy said, sitting down next to her and rubbing her back soothingly. 'You're exhausted—come on, let's get you into a gown and into bed, and let us take care of you.'

'It's all my fault, I shouldn't have let him talk me into it, we should have waited and now the baby's going to be too early,' she sobbed. Oh, she could understand the guilt all too well, but thirty-four weeks wasn't too early. Not like eighteen weeks...

'It's not your fault,' she said with a calm she didn't feel, 'and thirty-four weeks is quite manageable if it comes to that. It may well not. Come on, chin up, and let's find out what's going on.'

She handed Helen a gown, then left her alone for a few minutes to change and do a urine sample while she took the time to get her emotions back in order. What was the *matter* with her? She didn't think about her baby at all, normally. It was seeing that picture of Daisy's baby, and thinking about Matt again—always Matt.

She pulled herself together and went back to Helen. This was her first pregnancy, it had been utterly straightforward and uncomplicated to this point, and there was no reason to suspect that anything would go wrong even if she did give birth early. The baby was moving normally, its heartbeat was loud and strong, and Helen relaxed visibly when she heard it.

'Oh, that's so reassuring,' she said, her eyes filling, and she was still caressing her bump with a gentle, contented smile on her face when Ben arrived.

'OK, Helen, let's have a look at this baby and see how we're doing,' he said, and Amy watched the monitor.

The baby was a good size for her dates, there was no thinning of Helen's uterus as yet, and her contractions might well stop at this point, if she was lucky. Not everyone was.

She sucked in a breath and stepped back, and Ben glanced up at her and frowned.

'You OK?'

'Just giving you a bit more room,' she lied.

He grunted. It was a sound she understood. Matt used to do the same thing when he knew she was lying. Maybe they were more alike than she'd realised.

'Right, Helen, I'm happy with that. We'll monitor you, but I'm pretty sure they're just Braxton Hicks' and this will all settle down. We'll give you drugs to halt it if we can and steroids to mature the baby's lungs just to be on the safe side, and then if it's all stable and there's no change overnight, you can go home tomorrow.'

She swallowed. 'That's so reassuring. Thanks. I feel an idiot now, but I didn't know what to do.'

'Don't worry, you've done the right thing coming in,' Amy assured her. 'Why don't you try and have a sleep? I might have to disturb you from time to time, but I think a rest will do you good.'

She followed Ben out into the corridor. 'Any special instructions?'

'Yes. Come for dinner. Daisy's worried about you—she thinks the scan upset you.'

She forced a smile. 'Don't be silly, of course it didn't.'

That grunt again. 'Humour her, Amy, for my sake if nothing else. You know what she's like when she's got a bee in her bonnet about something. So—seven o'clock all right?'

She wasn't going to get out of it without a fuss, Amy realised, so she gave in. 'Seven will be fine. I'll see you there—and I'll keep you up to speed with Helen in the meantime.'

She picked up some flowers for Daisy from the super-market on her way home. And it really did feel like home, she thought as she showered and dressed.

Odd, how easily she'd settled into the little house, but she'd been lucky it had been available. Or maybe they'd deliberately kept it that way? She had a feeling they weren't exactly busting a gut to get a tenant and she wouldn't have put it past them to have caused the jinx in her boiler, but not even Daisy could make something rust through with the sheer force of her will.

It was a pity it was only temporary, but with their baby coming—well, thrilled though she was for them, it would be hard enough seeing Ben at work strutting around and showing off photos, without having it rammed down her throat at home.

At seven o'clock on the dot, she went out of the front door, stepped over the little low iron fence between the front gardens and rang their doorbell, and Daisy opened it instantly.

'Oh, flowers, thank you! Oh, you shouldn't,' Daisy said, hugging her as she stepped inside. 'I'm *so* glad you've come. I really thought I'd upset you…'

Her eyes were filling, and Amy sighed and hugged her back. 'Don't be silly. It was lovely seeing the picture and I'm really glad everything's all right.' She eased away and sniffed the air. 'Gosh, something smells wonderful. I've been starving recently. I think it's the cold, but I'm going to have to stop it. People keep bringing chocolates in.'

'Oh, tell me about it!' Daisy laughed. 'Come on through. Ben's cooking up a storm in the kitchen. He says it's a warming winter casserole, but all I know is it's taking a long time!'

It was delicious, and she would have eaten more, but her jeans were too tight and they were putting pressure on her bladder. That would teach her to stuff the patients' chocolates, she thought.

They cleared the table, and she excused herself and went up to the bathroom, but then had to hunt for toilet paper in the little cupboard under the sink.

A box fell out onto the floor, a slim rectangular box. She picked it up to put it back, and then stopped.

A pregnancy test, one of a twin pack…

Everything seemed to slow down for a moment, and then her heart lurched and started to race.

No. Don't be silly. You can't be.

Or could she? She'd thought her jeans were tight because she'd been such a pig recently, but she was feeling bloated—and her period was overdue. Only by a day, but the others…

'Amy? I've just remembered the loo paper's run out. I've got some here, I meant to bring it up.'

She opened the door, the pregnancy test in her hand, and Daisy stared down at it, her jaw dropping.

'Amy?' she murmured.

'I—um—I was looking for loo paper, and it fell out, and—Daisy, what if I'm…?'

She looked into Daisy's worried eyes, unable to say the word, but it hung there in the air between them.

'What makes you think you could be? I thought you were on the Pill? I mean, surely you've had periods?'

'Yes.' Yes, of course she had. Thank God. She leant against the wall, weak with relief. She'd just overeaten.

'And you weren't ill, were you, before the wedding?'

Ill? Alarm bells began to ring again. Not *ill*, exactly, but thinking back she'd been sick in the morning with the thought of seeing Matt, and her stomach had played up all the previous week with nerves. And it was only a low-dose pill, so timing was crucial if you were using it for contraception—which she wasn't, so maybe she'd just taken it for granted. What if…?

'I can't be, Daisy, it was only one night, and I've had three periods…' She trailed off.

Scant ones. Lighter than normal. Shorter—and this one was late.

Oh, how could she have been so dense? The signs were all there.

'Just use the pregnancy test,' Daisy offered tentatively, putting it back in her hand. 'It's going begging, and it would answer the question.'

Did she want it answered? The wedding was months ago, so she'd be almost 16 weeks—four weeks behind Daisy. Only two weeks to…

She felt bile rising in her throat again, and swallowed hard. 'Um…'

'Go on. I'll wait outside.'

She left the door open a crack, and the moment the loo flushed, she was back in there, holding Amy's hand while they stared at the little window. One line—then the other. Clear as a bell.

Amy sat down on the floor as if her strings had been cut, just as Ben appeared in the doorway behind Daisy. 'Are you girls OK?' he asked, looking from one to the other, and then he glanced down and saw the pregnancy test in Amy's lifeless hand, and she saw the penny drop.

'Oh, Amy,' he said softly, and as she stared at him blankly, the reality of her situation sank in and she began to shake.

'Ben, I can't—I can't do this again,' she said, her voice shuddering as fear engulfed her. 'Tell me I don't have to do this again! I can't—I'm so scared. No, please, no, not again, I can't...'

'Amy, shhh, it's OK,' Daisy said, gathering her up in her arms and rocking her against her chest. 'Hush now, sweetheart, it's all right, we'll take care of you. Don't be scared, it'll be all right.'

But it wasn't all right, and it wouldn't be, not ever again, she thought hysterically. She could hear herself gibbering, feel the panic and terror clawing at her, and underneath it, below it all, the agonising grief for the baby she'd loved and lost, too small to have any hope of surviving, and yet so much loved, so infinitely pre-cious, so perfect—so agonisingly, dreadfully missed.

Her empty arms ached to hold him, her soul wept for his loss. Every Christmas, every birthday, every anni-versary of the miscarriage—each one branded on her heart.

She couldn't bear it if it happened again...

They ended up in a row propped against the bath-room wall, her in the middle, Ben on one side, Daisy on the other, both of them holding her as she tried so very hard to push it all back down where it belonged.

And finally it was back there, safely locked away in the deepest recesses of her broken heart, and she could breathe again. Just about.

Ben let her go and shifted so he could see her face. 'Do you want me to help you tell him?' he asked, and she felt her eyes widen in shock.

Matt! Matt, who'd withdrawn into himself and iso-lated her in her grief, and then left her to deal with the loss of their baby alone. She hadn't even given him a thought, but—

'No! No, you can't!' she said frantically, clutching at Ben. 'I don't want him to know!'

Ben frowned. 'Well, of course he has to know, Amy, it's his baby. He needs to know—and you'll need him with you for all sorts of reasons. He should take some responsibility for this. He should have known better than to get you pregnant. I could kill him.'

She shook her head and drew her legs up, hugging her knees. 'No. Ben, I was on the Pill, I told him that. It's not his fault—not his responsibility. And I don't need him. I won't rely on him ever again, I can't. If anything goes wrong...'

'It won't.'

'It might! Ben, please! He can't deal with it, and I can't cope with all that again. I'd rather do it alone. You mustn't tell him. Please, Ben, promise me you won't tell him.'

Ben closed his eyes and let his breath out on a harsh sigh. For an age he said nothing, then he opened his eyes again and nodded. 'OK. I don't agree with you, and I think he should know, but I won't tell him yet—but you *have* to tell him at some point, Amy. He has the right to know—and the sooner the better.'

She opened her mouth to argue, but then shut it. She had the pregnancy to get through yet, and that was by no means a foregone conclusion.

'I'll tell him when it's over,' she said woodenly. 'Either way.'

'Amy, just because you've lost a baby in the past doesn't mean you're going to lose this one,' Ben said firmly, but he didn't understand. He hadn't been there, and even if he had...

'You can't say that. We didn't know why it happened, it could have been anything,' she told him, not sure what Matt had told him but needing to explain, to him and to Daisy, too, because she'd never really told her what had happened. 'I was eighteen weeks pregnant, I was fit and well, there was no bleeding, no pain, nothing, and the baby was...'

She shut her eyes tight. Perfect. Beautiful. And just too small, too frail, too unready for the world. She couldn't say it, couldn't let herself picture him, couldn't go back there.

As if he understood, Ben took her hands in his and held them firmly. 'We'll look after you. I'll get your old notes sent, and we'll make sure you're OK. We'll watch you like a hawk.'

'I was in Harrogate,' she said, her voice clogged with tears. 'With Matt—planning the wedding...'

He nodded. 'I know. Don't worry, Amy. We'll take care of you—but there's one condition.'

'I *can't* tell him yet!'

'It's not that, it's about you. You stay next door, so we can look after you properly and be there for you, or I *will* tell him. That's the deal,' he said flatly, and she looked into his eyes—Matt's eyes—and gave in. There was no arguing with the Walker men when they had that look in their eyes. And anyway, the last thing she wanted was to be alone in this, whatever she might have said.

'OK,' she agreed shakily. 'And I will tell him, but in my own way, in my own time. He'll smother me, and I can't cope with it yet. I just need to get through the next few weeks.'

Just until the baby was viable.

She couldn't say the words, but they understood, and Ben hugged her briefly and pulled her to her feet.

'I'll let you tell him. And I'll look after you. We'll look after you. It'll be OK.'

She smiled at him, feeling some of the terror dissipating in the friendly face of their support. She wasn't alone. And Ben and Daisy wouldn't desert her. So maybe she could do this, after all...

'So how are things?'

'Oh, you know how it is,' Ben said. 'How about you?'

Matt frowned. His brother sounded evasive. Odd, in only a handful of words over the telephone, but there was something there, something guarded. Something he wasn't telling him.

'Ditto. How's Daisy?'

'Better. Growing,' he said. 'She's finally stopped being sick and she's looking well. We did her twenty-week scan and everything's fine.'

'And Amy?' he asked carefully, and there was a pause.

'Amy's fine,' Ben replied, and he definitely sounded guarded now. So it wasn't that Ben was walking round him on eggshells because of Daisy being pregnant. It was Amy who was the problem.

'She—uh—she didn't want to see me again,' he admitted softly.

Matt heard Ben let out a soft sigh. 'Yeah. Well, she doesn't seem to have changed her mind. I'm sorry.'

Well, that was him told. He swallowed hard, staring sightlessly out of his sitting room window at the bleak winter garden of his small mews cottage. It had taken a bit of winding himself up to ask after her, and he wished he hadn't bothered.

Hell, he should just forget about her and move on, as she'd said, but…

'Look af—' His voice cracked a little, and he cleared his throat. 'Look after her for me.'

'We are. She's moved in next door, actually, into Daisy's house. Her boiler broke and it seemed to make sense.'

He had the totally irrational urge to jump in the car and come up and visit them. She'd be next door, just through the wall, and if he listened he'd hear her moving around—

Idiot. 'Give her my love,' he said gruffly. 'And Daisy and Florence. I'll try and see you sometime in the next couple of weeks. What are you doing over Christmas?'

'I don't know. I had thought we might go to Yorkshire, but I'm working. What about you?'

'I'm working Christmas Day and Boxing Day,' he said, and had a sudden longing for his mother's home cooking and his father's quiet, sage advice. But in the absence of that... 'Look, I've got to go, but I might try and get up between Christmas and New Year. Maybe on the twenty-seventh.'

'That'd be good. Let's see how it goes.'

'OK. You take care.'

'And you.'

He ended the call and watched a blackbird scratching in the fallen leaves under the bird feeder. Winter was setting in, the nights cold and frosty, even here in London.

He turned the television on and put his feet up, but he couldn't rest. Talking about Amy had unsettled him, and he'd suggested going up there—to see her?

Idiot. Idiot! It had taken him weeks to get over seeing her last time, so why on earth did he think it would be a good idea to go up to Yoxburgh in the hope of seeing her again?

He must be nuts. What the hell did he hope to achieve?

Maybe she's pregnant.

He stamped on that one hard. If she was pregnant, she would have told him weeks ago. Or Ben would. Yeah, Ben definitely would. Anyway, she was on the Pill, and she'd probably moved on, got herself another lover. He ignored the burn of acid at the thought. Maybe he should do the same, he told himself firmly. There was a new midwife who'd been flirting with him the past few weeks. He could take her out for dinner, see where it went.

But she's not Amy.

'You've lost Amy, get over it,' he growled. He had work he could do at the hospital, and anything was better than sitting here going over this again and again and again, so he turned the television off again, pulled on his coat and headed out of the door.

'Matt sends you his love.'

Amy felt herself stiffen. 'You didn't tell him?'

'No, of course I didn't tell him. I promised you I wouldn't.'

She let her breath out, and asked the question she'd been longing to ask. 'How is he?'

'OK, I think. We didn't talk for long. He asked how you were.'

'And what did you say?'

He smiled wryly. 'I told him you were fine and didn't want to see him again.'

It wasn't quite true. She'd been thinking about little else for the past two days, but he was right, she didn't want to see him again at the moment, because if she did, she'd have to tell him, and then...

'We were talking about Christmas,' Ben went on. 'We're both working on Christmas Day and we've got Florence on Boxing Day, but he might come up afterwards. What are you doing?'

He might come up afterwards...

'I haven't decided. They want me to work, so I'll probably do the day shift—'

'So spend Christmas night with us,' Daisy urged. 'We'll have a great time.'

It was tempting, but she shook her head. 'You want to be on your own—it's the last time you'll be able to. I'll be fine, really. Christmas Day is usually a lovely shift.'

And it would stop her worrying about her baby.

Ben scanned her the next day. They'd gone down to the big scanner in a quiet moment, and for the first time she actually acknowledged her baby's existence, dared to think about it, to see it as a real baby.

She watched the beating heart, saw the little arms and legs flailing around wildly, counted hands and feet, saw the fine, delicate column of its spine, the bridge of its nose, the placenta firmly fixed near the top of her uterus.

My baby, she thought, reaching out her hand and touching the image tenderly, and through her tears, she smiled at it and fell in love.

She pressed her hand to her mouth and closed her eyes as Ben turned off the scanner. 'Thank you,' she murmured.

'My pleasure,' he said, his voice roughened, and she realised he was moved, too, because this was his brother's baby, and he must have felt the loss of their first one keenly for Matt.

'Did you take a photo?' she asked, not sure she could bear to look at it. She still had the photo—

'Of course I did. I took one for us, as well, and one for Matt. To give him later,' he added hastily when she frowned.

She nodded. 'Thank you,' she said again, and took the tissue from him to wipe the gloop off her tummy. She'd started to show already, she realised. No wonder her jeans were tight.

Just eleven more days to go...

'You aren't going to lose this baby, Amy,' Ben said firmly, as if he'd read her mind. 'I'm not going to let you.'

'You may not be able to stop it.'

'I'd like to scan your cervix weekly from now on. Matt seemed to think—'

'Have you been talking to him?' she asked, horrified, but he shook his head.

'No. No, of course not. I promised I wouldn't. This was years ago, the only time we've talked about it. It was right after you lost the baby, and he was distraught. He thought it was your cervix. He was talking about monitoring you much more closely for the next pregnancy.'

She swung her legs down off the edge of the couch and stood up, straightening her clothes automatically. 'What next pregnancy?' she asked—fairly ridiculously, under the circumstances, she thought with a touch of hysteria, but if it hadn't been for the wedding she wouldn't have seen him again. 'He walked away, Ben. I told him I couldn't cope, that I needed time to get over it, and he walked away. He almost seemed relieved.'

'Amy, you're wrong,' he said, frowning, but she knew she wasn't. He'd been cold, remote. He'd hardly talked to her. He'd grieved for the baby, but he hadn't been able to support her, and he had rebuffed any attempt by her to support him.

'Ben, drop it. Please. You weren't there, you didn't see him. You can monitor me as closely as you like, but if it's all the same with you I'll take it one day at a time. I refuse to get my hopes up.'

'Because you feel guilty?'

She stared at him. Did she? Was that the reason she'd been so slow to realise that she was pregnant, and so reluctant to recognise this child? Because she didn't feel she deserved it? Because she'd gone for that walk with Matt the day before, and got overtired and then—?

'Ben, can we leave this?' she asked a little desperately, shutting the memories away before they could swamp her.

'Sure. I'm sorry. Here, your photo.' He handed her the little image in its white card mount, and she slipped it into her bag.

'I'd better get back to work. And—thank you, Ben. I really do appreciate all you're doing for me.'

'Don't mention it.'

She was doing fine.

There was nothing—nothing at all, from any test or examination—to indicate that she might lose this baby. Just as there hadn't been last time.

She put it out of her mind, and carried on as if nothing was any different. Apart from taking the usual precautions and supplements, she carried on as normal and tried not to think about it—or Matt—too much.

She worked the day shift on Christmas Day, and in the end she went round to Ben and Daisy's in the evening, just to eat. She didn't stay long, though. Daisy was looking tired, and it was their last Christmas alone together, so she left them to it after they'd eaten, and went home and thought about Matt.

Was he alone? It was all right for her, she'd had a great day at work, and she'd had a lovely dinner with Ben and Daisy. But Matt—who did he have?

She could phone him. Say Happy Christmas, and tell him he was going to be a father.

No. It was still too early, but she would tell him soon. She would.

CHAPTER FOUR

HE STOOD on the pavement outside, staring at the front door of Daisy's house and fighting indecision.

Amy was in. He could see the light from the kitchen shining down the hall, and he saw a shadow move across as if she'd walked into the dining room. She wasn't expecting him—none of them were, and he could see from the lack of lights that Ben and Daisy were out. So—to knock, or not to knock?

Instinct told him he wouldn't be welcome. Need told him to knock on the door anyway, to give her the benefit of the doubt, to try again, just one more time, to see if he could convince her to give their relationship another go.

He still hesitated, then with a sharp shake of his head, he walked firmly up the path and rapped on the door.

'Amy, it's Matt.'

Why had he done that? If he'd kept quiet, she would have come to the door, but instead there was silence. He resisted the urge to bend down and peer through the letter box. She was entitled to ignore him if she wanted to, and anyway there was a holly wreath hanging over it and it would probably stab him in the eye.

But she didn't ignore him. The porch light came on,

and he heard footsteps and the door swung inwards to reveal her standing there unsmiling.

'Hello, Matt,' she said quietly, and his heart turned over.

She looked—gorgeous. Her grey eyes were wary, her fair hair scrunched back in a ponytail as if she'd only just finished work and she was dressed in some shape-less rag of a jumper, but she looked warm and cosy and very, very dear, and he wanted to haul her into his arms and hold her.

As if she knew it, she hugged her arms defensively, so he forced himself to make do with a smile. 'Hi, there. Happy Christmas—or should that be Happy New Year?'

She ignored both. 'I didn't think Ben and Daisy were expecting you,' she said, her voice a little tight. 'You hadn't rung to confirm.'

'No. It was only tentative—a spur-of-the-moment thing.' Very spur of the moment. Two hours ago he'd been sitting in his house staring at the bird feeder and trying to talk himself out of it. He probably should have done.

'Oh. Well, they're out.'

'Will they be long?' Hell, they were talking like strangers.

'I don't know—why don't you come in? You can't stand out there for hours.'

'Will they be hours?' he asked, following her down the hall and eyeing her bottom thoughtfully. Had she put on a little weight? He thought so. It suited her.

'I don't know. Possibly. They're looking at baby stuff in the sales.'

Why had she said that? Why bring it up? She could have kicked herself, because absolutely the *last* thing she wanted to talk about with Matt was babies, although she knew that conversation was coming sometime soon.

'I was just making tea. Do you want some?'

'Yeah, that would be good. Thank you.'

So formal. So polite and distant. If he had any idea…

'You look well.'

She felt heat climb her cheeks. 'I am well.' *Very well, and pregnant with your child.* 'Have you eaten?'

'Yes—I had lunch, but don't mind me if you haven't.'

The stilted conversation was going to make her scream, but what was the alternative? *'Oh, incidentally, while I think of it, I'm having your baby'* didn't seem quite the right opener!

And anyway, she wasn't past the danger point yet. A few more days, maybe weeks—perhaps then.

She set a mug of tea down in front of him at the table, and finished making herself a sandwich. She was still starving, still eating anything she could lay her hands on—

'I thought you hated peanut butter?'

Damn. Trust him to notice. The only time she'd eaten it had been when she was pregnant, and any second now he'd guess.

'It goes in phases,' she said truthfully, and sat in a chair across the table and up from him, so she didn't have to look straight at him, didn't have to meet those searching blue eyes and risk blurting out the truth.

He gave a soft sigh and leant back. 'I'm sorry, I should have called you, but I thought you'd probably tell me to go to hell.'

'So why come?'

His smile was wry and rather sad. 'Why do you think, Amy?' he asked softly, and she swallowed.

'I don't— Matt, I told you before…'

He sighed softly. 'I know. That night was just for old times' sake. Laying our love to rest, I guess. I'd hoped it might turn out to be more than that. Might still turn out to be more.'

Oh, so much more. You have no idea.

'Matt, we've talked about this. We clearly didn't have what it takes, and if—'

She broke off, wary of straying into dangerous territory, but Matt had no such fear.

'If you hadn't got pregnant, our relationship would have fizzled out?'

Fizzled out? She'd said she couldn't cope with the wedding so soon after she'd lost her baby, and he'd heaved a sigh of relief and cancelled their entire relationship, so—yes, clearly he would have lost interest sooner or later, if he hadn't already done so.

She shrugged, and he shook his head slowly and gave a rueful smile.

'OK. I get that you think that, even if I don't agree, but—you seemed keen enough at the wedding, so what changed?'

What changed? *What changed?* She nearly laughed out loud at that. 'At the wedding I'd had a bit too much to drink,' she said bluntly, 'or I wouldn't have done anything so stupid. I would have thought better of it.'

'I've thought about very little since,' he said softly, and her heart contracted.

Oh, Matt.

She opened her mouth to tell him, but bottled out and changed the subject, asking instead how his parents were.

He gave a knowing little smile and let it go. 'Fine.

They've got snow up there at the moment, but they're OK, they've got plenty of food in and Dad can still get to the farms for emergencies, but it's supposed to be thawing this week.'

Oh, for God's sake, just tell her you love her! Tell her you want her! Tell her you want to try again, and this time you'll make it work. She's said we didn't have what it takes, but does anybody? For what happened to us, does anybody have what it takes?

He was opening his mouth when there was a sharp knock on the door. She got up and opened it, and he heard her murmur his name as Ben strode in.

'You were going to phone!' he said, hugging him and slapping his back. 'Come on, let's get you out of Amy's hair and you can give me a hand to unload the car. Daisy's been shopping with a vengeance.'

Maybe he didn't want to go? Maybe Amy was happy with him there? Maybe he hadn't finished what he'd come for?

But then he looked at her, composed, controlled but not exactly overjoyed, and he let out his breath on a quiet sigh and moved towards the door.

'Sure. Thanks for the tea, Amy. It was good to see you again.'

She smiled, but it didn't reach her eyes. 'Happy New Year, Matt.'

And she shut the door gently but firmly behind them, and went back to the table, her hands shaking.

She had to tell him sometime. Why not now? Why on earth hadn't she taken the opportunity?

She sighed. She knew why—knew that until this week was over, at least, she couldn't share it with him, but she would tell him. Ben was right, he needed to know, and she wanted their child to have him in its life. He was a good man, and he'd be a wonderful father.

What she couldn't deal with again, if anything went wrong, was his grief on top of her own.

No. Better not to have told him yet—and Ben had promised not to. She just hoped she could rely on him.

He was there until the following evening, and she spent as much time as possible at the hospital.

It wasn't hard. They were busy and short-staffed, and delighted to have her.

She'd put herself down for the night shift on New Year's Eve—better to keep busy, because she was eighteen weeks on that day, and if she hadn't been busy she would have gone out of her mind.

Her phone beeped a couple of times—Happy New Year messages from people, she thought, but she was too busy to check it, so she carried on filling in the notes and went back to her mums to check on them.

But when her night shift finished and she went home in the cold, bright crisp air of the morning, she finally checked her phone and found a text from a friend and a voicemail message.

From Matt.

'Hi, Amy, it's Matt. Sorry to miss you, I expect you're working. I just wanted to say Happy New Year, and it was good to see you again the other day. I'm sorry it was so brief. Maybe next time...' There was a pause, then he added, 'Well, you know where I am if you want me.'

If she wanted him?

She sat down on the sofa in her sitting room, and

played his hesitant, reluctant message again and again and again.

Of course she wanted him. She wanted him so much it was unbearable, today of all days, the exact stage to the day that she'd lost their first baby. She laid her hand over the tidy little bump—hardly a bump at all. If you didn't know, you wouldn't guess, but assuming it made it, and it was a big assumption, this baby was going to cause havoc in her life.

And in Matt's.

She had to tell him. Ben was right, she couldn't just keep relying on them, and he had the right to know about his child. She took the two-week-old scan photo out of her bag and stared at it, tracing the tiny face with her finger. It would be bigger now. As big as Samuel...

Lord, even the name hurt. She sucked in a breath, the images crowding in on her—the midwife's eyes so full of compassion as she wrapped his tiny body in a blanket and placed it in Matt's arms. The tears in his eyes, the searing agony she could see in every line of his body as he stared down at his son.

He'd lifted the baby to his lips, kissed his tiny head, shuddered with grief. It had broken him—broken both of them—and their relationship, like their son, had been too fragile, too young to survive.

She almost rang him. Her finger hovered over the call button, but then she turned the phone off and told herself to stop being so ridiculous. She'd decided not to tell him until after the twenty-week scan. Maybe longer. Maybe not until it was viable. He'd been so gutted last time, so deeply distressed, that he'd been unreachable, and she knew—she just *knew*—he'd be a nightmare if she told him. He'd probably have her admitted so he could scan her three times a day, but she wasn't having any of it. It was utterly unnecessary, and thinking about it all the time just made it all so much worse.

So she didn't ring him, and then she was past the time of the miscarriage, into the nineteenth week. Then the twentieth, and the big scan, which she could hardly bear to look at she was so nervous.

But it was normal, and it looked much more like a baby now, every feature clearly defined. It was sucking its thumb, and Amy felt a huge tug of love towards this tiny, vulnerable child—Matt's child. 'Do you want to know what it is?' the ultrasonographer asked her, but she shook her head.

'No.' Knowing would make it harder to remain detached, and she'd been careful not to look—but the baby was moving vigorously, and she could feel it all the time now, so real, so alive, so very, very strong that finally, at last, she began to allow a tiny glimmer of hope to emerge.

Was it possible that this baby would be all right?

She wanted to share it, to tell everyone in the world, but she was still a little afraid she might jinx it, so she took the photo home, propped it up on the bedside table next to her so she could see it when she woke, and fell asleep with a smile on her face and her hand curved protectively over her child...

She went shopping the following week with Daisy, and she talked Amy into getting some pretty clothes.

'You can't just wear scrubs and jog bottoms and baggy jumpers for the rest of your pregnancy,' she scolded, and handed her all sorts of things, all of which Amy thought made her look shockingly pregnant.

Shockingly, because she'd still not really taken it on board. It was still too early, the baby wasn't yet viable, and she felt a little quiver of nerves.

'Daisy, I really don't think—'

'No. Don't think. You think altogether too much. You're fine, Amy. You're well. Everything's OK.'

'I was well last time,' she said woodenly, and Daisy dropped the clothes she was carrying and hugged her.

'Oh, sweetheart, you'll be fine. Come on, Ben says everything's looking really good. It's time to be happy.'

Happy? Maybe, she thought, as Daisy took her to a café and plied her with hot chocolate and common sense, and gradually she relaxed. She was being silly. She could buy a few clothes—just enough. That wasn't tempting fate, was it? And her bras *were* strangling her. They finished their hot chocolate and went back to the shops.

And gradually, as the weeks passed and she got nearer to her due date, she began to dare to believe it might all be all right. She was beginning to feel excited, to look forward to the birth—except, of course, she'd be alone.

Unless she told Matt.

She felt her stomach knot at the thought. It was the beginning of April and Daisy had just started her maternity leave, five weeks before her baby was due, and nine weeks before Amy's. Gosh, 31 weeks, Amy thought, stunned, and bit her lip. There was no excuse now not to tell him and she was being unfair. He'd need time to get his head round it, and he was going to give her hell for keeping it quiet, but it had gone on for so long now that she wasn't sure how to broach the subject.

The baby was kicking her vigorously all night now.

She'd never felt Samuel move—well, maybe a flutter, just before the end, but not like this, not so you could see it from the outside.

Matt would love to feel it…

Oh, how to tell him? Because she knew she had to, knew he had a right to know, and she was sharing the things she should have been sharing with him with Ben and Daisy, so much so that it was unfair.

Just how unfair was brought home to her two weeks later, when she was in their nursery looking at all the baby things and she'd jokingly talked about Ben delivering her and asked Daisy if she could borrow him. They exchanged a glance, and Ben sighed softly. 'Amy, I'm not my brother,' he said, his voice gentle. 'I'm happy to help, you know that, but it isn't me you need, and I can't take his place. And it isn't fair of you to ask me to. It isn't fair on any of us, especially not Matt.'

She felt hot colour flood her face, and turned blindly and went out of the room, stumbling downstairs and out into the garden. She hadn't thought of it from his side, but of course it was an imposition, and she'd been thoughtless, taken Ben and Daisy for granted, cheated Matt—but—

'Amy, wait!'

He stopped her just before she went through the gate in the fence, his hand on her arm gentle but firm.

'Amy. Please don't walk away. I don't mean to hurt you, but it's not my baby, sweetheart. Your baby needs its proper father—and he needs to know.'

She nodded, scrubbing away the tears. 'You're right. I know you're right. I'll do it soon, I promise. I'm just being silly. I just don't know how…'

'Do you want me to help you?'

She shook her head. 'No. I'll do it. I'll call him.'

'Promise me?'

She nodded, swallowing a sob. 'I promise.'

She escaped then, and let herself into her house and cried her heart out in the conservatory where they couldn't hear her through the wall.

She was mortified, but more than that, she was afraid. She'd been leaning on Ben, she realised, not only because he was Matt's twin, but because he was reliable and kind and generous and decent, and because he'd let her.

And all the time it had been Matt she'd wanted, Matt she'd needed, Matt she still needed and always would. But this baby was going to make life so complicated, and it dawned on her in a moment of clarity that she'd been stalling because the status quo was far easier to deal with than the reality of sharing a child with a man who didn't really love her, even if he liked to think he might.

And that, she realised at last, was at the heart of her reluctance. They'd had a great time together at first, and the sex had always been brilliant, but Matt didn't love her, not enough to cope with the worst things life could thrust at them, and she didn't want him doing what he'd done before and offering to marry her just because they were having a child.

No, that was wrong, they'd already talked about marriage last time, made half-plans for the future. He hadn't officially proposed, but they were heading that way, drifting into it, and she wondered if they would have drifted all the way to a wedding if she hadn't got pregnant. But she had, of course, because they'd been careless with contraception on the grounds that it wouldn't have been a disaster if she'd got pregnant, at the time they'd both been anticipating a future together

Except it had been—a disaster that had left shock-waves still rippling around her life now over four years later.

She went round to see Daisy the following day and apologised for being an idiot, and they both ended up in tears. She talked about Matt, about how she felt, and then looked at all the stuff in the nursery and felt utterly overwhelmed.

She was having this baby in just seven weeks, maybe less, and she'd been so busy fretting about Matt she'd done nothing to prepare for it. 'I need to go and buy some basics,' she said to Daisy, and she rolled her eyes.

'Finally! Otherwise you know what'll happen, you'll have it two weeks early and you'll have no baby stuff at all!'

She was wrong. It wasn't Amy who had her baby two weeks early, it was Daisy herself.

She'd come into the hospital on Wednesday morning to see them all because she was bored and restless and sick of housework, and she was sitting in the office chatting to Amy in a quiet moment when her eyes widened and then squeezed tight shut.

Then she gave an exasperated sigh. 'Oh, I can't believe I've been so *stupid*! I had backache all day yesterday, but I've been cleaning. The kitchen was absolutely pigging, and—Amy, this isn't funny, stop laughing at me and get Ben!'

'Get Ben why?' Ben asked, walking in, and then he looked at Daisy and his jaw dropped.

'What's the matter?' Amy teased with a grin. 'Never seen a woman in labour before?'

It was a textbook labour, if a little fast, and Amy made it quite clear to Ben that she was in control.

'You're on paternity leave as of now, so don't even think about interfering,' she told him as she checked Daisy between contractions. Her body was doing a wonderful job, and Amy was happy to let nature take its course.

It was just another delivery, her professional mask was in place, and she was doing fine until the baby was born, but once she'd lifted their son and laid him on Daisy's chest against her heart, she let Ben take over.

It was Ben who told her it was a boy, Ben who covered him with a warmed towel as Daisy said hello to their little son, Ben who cleared his mouth of mucus with a gentle finger and stimulated that first, heart-warming cry, because Amy was transfixed, her eyes flooded with tears, her whole body quivering.

She wanted Matt with her when she gave birth in a few weeks, Matt to take their baby from the midwife and lay him—her?—on her chest, and gaze down at them both with love and wonder in his eyes. If only things were different…

But they weren't different, they were what they were, and she'd be alone, not only for the delivery but for the whole business of motherhood, and her confidence suddenly deserted her.

I can't do it alone! I can't be that strong. I'm not that brave. Matt, why can't you love me enough? I need you—

No, she didn't! She stopped herself in her tracks, and

took a long, slow, steadying breath. She was getting way ahead of herself. One day at a time, she reminded herself. She was getting through her pregnancy like that. She could get through motherhood in the same way. The last thing she needed was a man who didn't love her enough to ride out the hard times, who when the crunch came would walk away, however much he might think he wanted her.

And right now, Daisy and Ben and their new little son were her priority.

'Let's give them a minute,' she said to Sue, the midwife assisting her, and stripping off her gloves, she turned and walked blindly out of the door and down the corridor to the stairwell.

Nobody would find her there. She could hide here for a minute, get herself together. Think about what Ben had said.

Should Matt be there with her when she gave birth? Even if they weren't together?

Yes, if it was like this, but if anything went wrong…

He'd been there last time, distant and unreachable, his eyes filled with pain. She couldn't cope with that again, couldn't handle his pain as well as her own. The last thing she needed during her labour was a man she couldn't rely on if anything went wrong, a man who couldn't talk about his feelings or hers.

But she needed him…

No! No, she didn't! She was made of sterner stuff than that, and she could cope alone. She could. She knew all the midwives here, she'd have plenty of support during her labour. She didn't need Matt.

She got to her feet and went back to them, to find Ben sitting in the chair cuddling his tiny son with a tender smile on his face that wasn't going to fade any time soon.

Lucky little boy, she thought. So, so lucky. Her baby would have a father who loved him like that, she knew, but it wouldn't have two parents sharing its life on a daily basis, supporting each other through thick and thin.

Her hand slid down over her baby in an unconscious caress. If only…

She helped Ben get the house ready after her shift finished at three.

He was bringing Daisy and Thomas home that evening, and they were almost done.

'Gosh, I've never seen it so clean and tidy,' she said with a laugh, and he just rolled his eyes and sighed.

'Silly girl. I should have smelled a rat when I got home last night and found the place sparkling. I can't believe I was so dense.' He gave the quilt cover one last tug into place, straightened up and met Amy's eyes.

'Matt should be with you when you have the baby, Amy. Labour can be a tough and lonely place. You're going to need support.'

'Ben, it's OK,' she said softly. 'I'll be all right.'

'And what about Matt? What about my brother, Amy? He lost a baby too, you know. He needs this to put things right for him, to balance the books a bit. You can't deny him the experience of seeing his child born. This is going to happen. You can't keep ignoring it.'

She swallowed and nodded. 'No. You're right, I know you're right. I'll discuss it with him when I tell him— just maybe not tonight. You'll want to talk to him tonight, tell him your news. There are things we'll need to sort out anyway, and I've only got five weeks to go. Nothing's going to go wrong now.'

Oh, foolish, foolish words.

She woke on Friday morning with a slight headache, and went downstairs and poured herself a tall glass of fruit juice and iced water, and sat in the conservatory listening to the birds.

Gosh, her head was thumping, she thought, and went and had a shower, washed her hair and let it air dry while she had another drink.

She must be dehydrated. Too busy yesterday to drink much. Too busy, and too stressed because Matt was coming up for the weekend and she was going to tell him. She'd tried to phone him last night from the hospital but she hadn't got hold of him, and she would have tried again when she got home, but she'd worked till nine and she'd been too tired, and today she was starting at seven. She'd try again this afternoon, before he left London—not that it seemed right to do it like that, over the phone, but she couldn't exactly do it face to face. He didn't need to be an obstetrician to work it out, so there'd be no subtlety, no putting it gently.

No 'You remember that night you made love to me, and I told you it was all right because I was on the Pill? Well, there's something I need to tell you.' Nothing so easy as that—although, to be fair, it couldn't be easier than just opening the door to him. That would be pretty straightforward, she thought with a wry grimace.

She dressed for work, wriggling her feet into her shoes and sighing because even they were getting tighter. Everything was, but it was pointless buying things at this stage.

It was ludicrously busy at work, of course, and she

began to think she ought to consider taking maternity leave sooner than she'd allowed.

She had two more weeks to go, come Monday, and she was working today and tomorrow. Just as well, since Matt was going to be around, although she'd have to talk to him face to face in the end.

She found time for lunch somewhere between one and two—a quick sandwich eaten on the run, which gave her vicious indigestion, but she needed something in her stomach so she could take some paracetamol for her headache.

She sat down in the office for a moment and eased her shoes off. Pregnancy was the pits, she decided, and vowed to be nicer to her mums when they complained about it in future. Really, men didn't know how lucky they were—and that's if they were even there!

No. She mustn't be unfair. She hadn't given Matt the chance to be there.

'Amy, can you come? I've got a mum about to deliver.'

'Sure.'

She squirmed her feet back into her shoes, winced and followed Angie, one of the other midwives, down the corridor to the delivery room. Roll on nine o'clock, she thought. Why on earth had she agreed to do a double shift? It was a good job Ben wasn't here to see her, or Daisy. They'd skin her, but there hadn't been anyone else available at the last minute and at least it would mean she'd be out when Matt arrived.

Any other day, she thought, and tried to smile brightly at their patient. 'Hiya, I'm Amy,' she said, and threw herself into the fray.

* * *

Matt's car was outside, and just the thought that he was there made her heart pound, her throat dry and her chest ache.

She hadn't been able to ring him that afternoon. Should she ring him tonight?

No. Tonight should be for Ben and Daisy, for him to meet his little nephew, although judging by the sounds coming through their front door, Thomas was well and truly met.

She could just picture him holding the tiny baby in those big, capable hands.

She closed her eyes to shut out the image and squeezed them tight shut. Oh, they ached. Everything ached. Her head, her eyes, her feet...

She looked down, and blinked. Her feet were swollen. Not just the normal swollen feet of pregnancy, but a more sinister kind of swollen. And her fingers felt tight, and her head was splitting. She could feel her heartbeat in her eyeballs, even, and as she mentally listed the symptoms, she closed her eyes and leant against her front door, stunned.

Pre-eclampsia? Just like that? But she'd been fine up to now. Ben had been monitoring her minute by minute until Thomas had been born, but that was only two days ago, and she'd had no symptoms at all.

Except the headache this morning, and the tight shoes and clothes, and the epigastric pain she'd put down to indigestion—

Lord, she felt dreadful.

Matt. I need Matt.

She could hear voices through their front door, and the baby was quiet now. If she called out— Oh, her head ached so much, and she moaned. It was so far to the door...

She stepped over the little fence, arm outstretched towards the bellpush, but then she stumbled and half fell, half slid down the door with a little yelp. Oh, her head. She heard a voice, heard running footsteps, then felt the door open as she slid sideways across the step and came to rest.

There was a startled exclamation, and gentle hands touched her face.

Matt...!

CHAPTER FIVE

'WHAT was that?'

Ben frowned at him. 'I don't know. Amy? Are you all right?' he called, and there was a muffled cry and a crash against the door.

'What the hell—?' Matt thrust his nephew at Daisy and ran down the hall, turning the door handle and then catching the door as it was forced inwards.

'Matt, she's...' Ben began, as the door swung open and Amy tumbled over at his feet.

He knelt beside her, cupping her face in his hand and turning her towards him so he could check her pupils.

The doctor in him was registering her symptoms. The man was in shock, and deeply, furiously angry, because Amy was pregnant, and none of them had told him—unless it wasn't his?

'It's yours,' he heard Ben say, but he didn't answer. He was too damned angry with him and too worried about Amy to deal with that now, and the fear just ramped up a notch.

'Amy? Amy, it's Matt, talk to me!' he said urgently, his eyes scanning her. How the hell had she got like this? Her feet were swollen, her face was puffy, her eyes—her eyes were opening, searching for him.

'Matt.' She lifted her hand and rested it against his cheek, and worry flickered in her eyes. 'I've been trying to phone you. I've got something I have to tell you.'

He laid his hand over hers and squeezed it. 'It's OK, sweetheart. Don't talk now.'

'But I have to. I have to tell you—'

'Amy, it's all right, I know about the baby. You just close your eyes and rest, let me look after you.'

Her fingers fluttered against his cheek, and he pressed his lips to her palm and folded her hand over to keep it safe. It made her smile, a weak, fragile smile that tore his heart wide open. 'I'm so glad you're here...'

'Me too,' he said softly, his voice choked, and turned his head. 'She's about to fit, we need an ambulance,' he snapped at Ben, but he'd gone and Daisy, standing there with Thomas in her arms and shock in her eyes, answered him.

'He's getting the car—he said there wasn't time for an ambulance. I'll get the emergency team to meet you there.'

'We'll need a theatre.'

'I know. Ben's outside with the car. You need to go.'

They did. She was barely conscious now, her eyes rolling back in her head, and he felt sick with fear. He scooped her up, ran down the path and got into the back of the car behind Ben, Amy on his lap.

Please be all right. Please let the baby be all right. Don't let it happen again. I can't do this again. Amy can't do this again. Please be all right...

They screeched into the hospital, pulled up outside Maternity and left the car there with the doors hanging open. Ben threw the keys at the reception clerk and asked her to deal with it, and a waiting team took over.

Matt dumped her on the trolley and they had her in the lift and on oxygen instantly, a line was going in each hand and an infusion of magnesium sulphate was started while they were still on the move.

'I'm scrubbing,' he said, and earned himself a hard stare.

'No way. By all means get gowned up, but I'm doing this, not you,' Ben said flatly, and filled the team in. 'Pre-eclampsia, sudden onset, partial loss of consciousness, she hasn't fitted as far as we know but she might have done,' he told them, but they were already on it, primed by Daisy, and as Ben went to scrub they were preparing her for surgery.

There was no job for Matt, so he stepped back out of the way. Someone fed his arms into a gown and tied it up, put a cap on his head, a mask over his face, and he stood there, his heart in his mouth, and watched as his brother brought his son into the world.

A boy. A perfect, beautiful boy, but still and silent, his body blue, his chest unmoving.

Please, no, not again...!

Matt was frozen to the spot, his eyes fixed on the little chest, begging it to move.

'Come on, baby,' the midwife was saying, sucking his mouth out, rubbing his back, flicking his feet. 'Come on, you can do it.'

When the cry came, he thought his legs would give way under him. He dragged in a huge breath, then another, and pressed his fist to his mouth to keep in the sob.

'Go and meet your baby,' Ben said gently, and he went over on legs that were not quite steady and reached out a finger and touched his baby's hand. Tiny, transparent pink fingers clenched around his fingertip, and another sob wrestled free from his chest.

He stroked the fingers, oh, so gently with his thumb, afraid for the fragile, friable skin, but he was past that stage. Thirty-five weeks was OK. He'd be OK. The relief, for a child he didn't even know he was having until half an hour ago, was enormous.

It had plagued him, all the what ifs, the regrets that not once but twice he'd let her send him away without putting up a fight, the hope that she might contact him and tell him she was pregnant that had flickered and then died. He'd even seen her at Christmas, thought she looked well, had even put on a little weight, for heaven's sake, and all the time...

He turned his head. 'How is she?' he asked hoarsely.

'Stable. We'll know more when she comes round. The neurologist is coming to have a look at her and we're moving her to Maternity HDU.'

He swallowed the fear and turned back to his son.

'Hello, my little man,' he murmured softly, his hands trembling but his voice gentle with reassurance. 'Your mummy's not very well, but she'll be OK, and so will you. Daddy's here now and I'm going nowhere,' he promised.

'Want to hold him?' the midwife asked gently.

He nodded, and she wrapped him in a soft cotton blanket and placed him in Matt's arms. 'He needs to go to SCBU for a while, just to make sure he's OK and his lungs are coping, but he's looking good so far. He's 2.1 kilos. That's a good weight for a preemie—over four and a half pounds.'

He nodded. He could feel him, knew he was a good size, but that wasn't what he was seeing.

He was seeing another child in his arms, far smaller, too small to make it in this world, a child he'd never had the chance to love. His heart ached with the love he'd never been able to give, would never be able to give that child, and now he had another child, a child whose mother might not recover from this. God, how much more—?

Ben appeared at his side, and he felt an arm around his shoulders. 'He's going to be all right, Matt,' he said softly, and there was a catch in his voice.

He nodded. 'He is. Ben, how did she get like this?'

'I have no idea. I've had her under a microscope, and I'll be going over her notes again with a fine-toothed comb, to see if there's anything I've missed, but she hasn't even had high blood pressure.'

'What is it now?'

'Two thirty-five over 170.'

'*What*?' He felt his legs buckle slightly and jammed his knees back hard. That was high. Too high. Ludicrously high. She could still fit, still end up with brain damage—

'Don't go there, Matt. She's in good hands.'

He nodded, handed the baby back to the midwife and turned to watch Amy being wheeled out of Theatre. 'I need to be with her.'

'Yes, you do. I'm sorry. If I hadn't been off on paternity leave for the past two days, I would have spotted this coming on. Someone's just told me she did a double shift today, and she was supposed to be working tomorrow.'

'That's crazy!' he said under his breath. 'What the hell was she thinking about? Or was she keeping out of my way?'

'I don't know,' Ben said heavily. 'She wasn't booked to do the double shift. I think they were short-staffed, but if I'd been here I wouldn't have let her do it.'

The anger, so carefully banked, broke free again. 'Nor would I, but I didn't get that choice, did I? Why didn't any of you tell me she was pregnant? How could you *keep* that from me? For God's sake, Ben, I'm your *brother*!'

They were following the trolley, and Ben paused and met his eyes. 'You think I don't know that? I've been trying to get her to tell you since the day she found out.'

'*You* could have told me.'

'No. I promised her I wouldn't. I said I'd look after her.'

He made a harsh sound in his throat. 'If you'd told me, I would have been looking after her, and this wouldn't have happened.'

'Oh, for God's sake, man, if you're that bothered, why did you let her go in the first place? And it wasn't me who got her pregnant,' Ben snapped impatiently, and with a rough sigh he stalked off after the trolley, leaving Matt to follow or not.

He followed, his thoughts reeling, and they walked the rest of the way in an uncomfortable silence.

She fitted in the night, and Matt stood at the end of the bed with his heart in his mouth while all hell broke loose and drugs were pumped into her and the team struggled to control her blood pressure.

He clenched his fists and forced himself to keep out of it, to let them do their jobs, but in fairness they were doing exactly what he would have done if he'd been in charge, so he watched the monitor, and he waited, and finally it started to come down as her kidneys kicked in again, and he watched the numbers on the monitor drop gradually to sensible levels.

He felt his own blood pressure slowly return to something in the normal range, and then once he could get near her again he sagged back into the chair beside the bed and took her puffy, bloated hand in his. He stroked the back of it gently with his thumb, the rhythm soothing him, the contact with her warmth giving him hope.

She'd survived, and she was breathing. For now, that was all he could think about. All he could let himself think about.

'It's OK, Amy,' he murmured, trying to inject some conviction into his voice. 'You'll be all right, my love. Just hang in there. I'm right here, and I'm not leaving. You'll be OK, don't worry. The baby's fine. He's going to be fine, and so are you...'

His voice cracked, and he broke off, dragging in a deep breath and staring up at the ceiling.

Who was he trying to convince? Her, or himself? Empty words, the sort of platitudes he heard desperate relatives telling their loved ones all the time in the face of insurmountable odds.

Were they insurmountable? He forced himself to be realistic. He treated women with pre-eclampsia all the time, and usually it was fine, but rarely—very rarely—it came on so fast, like Amy's, that it caught them by surprise, and then it could spiral out of control with shocking speed. Sometimes there were no symptoms at all, the woman went straight into eclampsia and began fitting, and then the symptoms might follow later.

The outcome then was dependent on many factors— what had caused the fit, what damage it had done, how bad the multi-system failure was—and it was impossible to second-guess it.

She might have had a stroke, or got irreversible kidney or liver damage, he thought, and stopped himself running through the list. He didn't need to borrow trouble. Time would tell, and until then he'd look on the bright side. She was alive. She was breathing for herself, her kidneys were starting to work again, her blood results were in the manageable range and he just had to wait. It often got worse before it got better. He knew that.

The time, though, seemed to stand still, punctuated only by the regular visits of the nursing and medical staff every few minutes until it all became a blur.

Underneath the worry for Amy, though, concern for the baby was nagging at him incessantly. All the staff were busy, but even so they'd given him a couple of reassuring updates. It wasn't the same as seeing him, though. He wanted to watch over him as he was watching over Amy, to will him to live, to tell him he loved him.

But Amy needed him more, so he sat there feeling torn in half, part of him desperate to go and see his tiny son, the other, bigger part unable to drag himself away from Amy's bedside until he was entirely confident of her recovery.

Then Ben came in, at some ungodly hour of the morning, and stood behind him, hands on his shoulders, the weight so reassuring, anchoring him, somehow.

'How is she?' he asked softly.

Matt shook his head.

'I don't know. She fitted. They couldn't get her blood pressure down for a while. It's down now, it's looking better but she's sedated at the moment. We've just got to wait.'

He felt Ben's hand squeeze his shoulder. 'I'm sorry.'

'Don't be,' he said, his voice clogged. 'It wasn't your fault, you weren't even supposed to be working. I was just stressed and I shouldn't have taken it out on you. I know it happens.'

'I'm still sorry. I should have made sure someone kept an eye on her. I should have done it myself.'

'No. If she was fine, you couldn't have foreseen this, and you know how quickly it can happen, and she's a midwife. She should have recognised the signs. As you say, it must have been really sudden.' He put his hand over Ben's and gripped it, leaning back against him, taking strength from his brother while he voiced his fears. 'What am I going to do if she's not all right?' he asked unevenly, and he felt Ben's hand tighten.

'She'll be all right. Have faith.'

He dropped his hand abruptly. 'Sorry. I don't have faith any longer. I used it all up last time.'

'This isn't like that.'

'No. No, it isn't. This time I've got the baby, and I might lose the woman I love. I don't know which is worse.'

'You won't lose her.'

'There's more than one way to lose someone, Ben. She might have brain damage.'

'She's responding to pain.'

'Earthworms respond to pain,' he said bluntly, and Ben sighed softly, letting go of his shoulders and moving away slightly, leaving him in a vacuum.

'Have you had a break yet? Gone for a walk, stretched your legs? Eaten anything?'

He shook his head. 'I don't want anything—except to know how the baby is.'

'He's doing well. I rang from home, and they said he's fine, he's breathing on his own and looking good. They've put a tube in and given him some colostrum from the milk bank and they're happy with him.'

He nodded, his eyes fixed on Amy, and felt a little more of the tension ease. He glanced at the clock, then up at his brother with a frown. 'It's the middle of the night. You should be with Daisy. She's only just given birth.'

'She's fine, and I've got my mobile. I promised I wouldn't be long, but I couldn't sleep, so I thought I'd come back and see how it was going, make sure you were OK. Get you to eat something, maybe.'

'I'm not hungry.'

'Come and see the baby, at least, then, to put your mind at rest. Amy's stable, and we won't be far away. They'll ring me if they want us.'

How did he know that only seeing him with his own eyes would be good enough?

Stupid question. His brother knew everything about him. He got to his feet, stiff and aching from the hard plastic chair, and walked the short distance to SCBU.

The last time he'd been in here was to see the Grieves twins, back in September. Now it was the end of April, and he was here to see his own child, experiencing at first hand the hope and fear felt by the parents of a premature baby.

He washed his hands thoroughly, doused them in alcohol gel and introduced himself to the staff.

The neonatal unit manager, Rachel, remembered him from September, and she smiled at him encouragingly.

'He's doing really well. Come and say hello,' she said, and led him over to the clear plastic crib.

Ben had left him to it, giving him space. He wasn't sure he wanted it, but he was talking to a woman in a dressing gown sitting tearfully by a crib, and he glanced across and winked at Matt.

You can do it. Go and say hello to your son.

He nodded, and took the last few steps to the side of the crib. He was used to seeing babies in them, but not *his* baby, and he blew his breath out slowly at the impact. He seemed so small, so vulnerable, so incredibly fragile.

It was quite irrational. As a twin specialist he was used to delivering babies much smaller than him, sometimes as much as nine weeks younger, on the very edge of viability, but age wasn't everything and their baby wasn't out of the woods yet, he knew.

'Hi, little guy,' he said softly, and threading his hands through the ports, he cradled his sleeping son's head tenderly with one hand, the other cupping the tiny, wrinkly little feet. They fascinated him. The toes were so tiny, the nails perfectly formed, the skinny little legs so frail and yet so strong.

He looked like Ben and Daisy's Thomas, he thought. Not surprisingly, since half their DNA pool was identical. They were practically half-brothers, he realised, and smiled. They'd grow up together, be friends. That was good.

He studied the tiny nose with its pinpoint white spots on the skin, the creased-up little eyes tight shut, the mouth working slightly. There was a tube up his nose taped to his cheek, and a clip on his finger leading to the monitor, but he didn't need to look at it. He watched the scrawny, ribby little chest going up and down, up and down as he breathed unaided, and felt more of the tension leave him.

He was a tiny, living miracle, and Matt swallowed a huge lump in his throat as he stared down at the sleeping baby.

'He's doing really well,' Rachel said matter-of-factly. 'We put the tube in to get his feeding off to a good start, because he's a little light for his dates, but he's great. Just a bit skinny, really.'

Matt nodded. He was. At a guess her placenta had been failing for a couple of weeks, and although he was a good size, he was still slightly behind what he should have been. Whatever, he'd catch up quickly enough now, and he was clearly in good hands.

'He's looking good,' Ben said quietly from beside him, and he nodded again. It seemed easier than talking, while his throat was clogged with emotion and his chest didn't seem to be working properly.

He eased away from the crib with a shaky sigh and, asking Rachel to keep in touch, he headed out of the unit with Ben.

'How about coming down to the canteen?'

'I want to get back to Amy,' he said, even though he could murder a drink, now he thought about it.

'Can I get you anything, then? Tea, coffee, bacon roll?'

'Coffee and a bacon roll would be good,' he said, but when it came he could hardly eat it. Sitting there outside the high dependency unit and fretting about Amy did nothing for the appetite, he discovered, and the bacon roll only brought back memories—the morning after the wedding, when he'd spent the night with her, trying to convey with actions rather than words how much he loved her; the mornings they'd woken in his London apartment and she'd snuggled up to him and told him she was hungry and he'd left her there, warm and sleepy, and made her breakfast.

They'd been halcyon days, but they'd ended abruptly when she'd lost Samuel.

Odd. He always thought of him as Samuel, although they'd never talked about it since that awful day. They'd talked about names before, argued endlessly about girls' names but agreed instantly on Sam.

He tipped his head back with a sigh, resting it against the wall behind the hard plastic chair in the waiting area outside the HDU. Ben had brought the bacon roll and coffee up to him and then gone back to Daisy and their own tiny baby, and now he sat there, staring at the roll in his hand while he remembered the past and wondered what the future held.

Once, it had seemed so bright, so cut and dried and full of joy. Now, over four years later, Amy was lying there motionless, possibly brain injured, their newborn son was in SCBU, and Matt had no idea what lay ahead for the three of them.

He swallowed the last of the cold coffee, threw the roll into the bin and went back to Amy's side. Could the sheer force of his willpower pull her through? He didn't know, but he'd give it a damn good try.

He picked up her lifeless hand, and stopped. Was he clutching at straws, or was it less swollen? He looked at it thoughtfully, wondering if he was imagining it. No. He didn't think so. It *was* improving, slowly. *She* was improving.

Shaking with relief, knowing it was still early days,

trying to find a balance between sheer blind optimism and drenching fear, he cradled the hand in his, pressed it to his cheek and closed his eyes.

She was floating.

No, not floating. Drowning. Drowning in thick, sticky fog and awash with pain.

There were noises—bleeps and tweets, hisses and sighs. People talking, alarms going off, laughter in the distance.

Hospital? It sounded like the hospital. Smelt like the hospital. But she was lying down, floating on the fog—or water? Drowning again. It felt like water—

She coughed, and felt her hand squeezed. Odd. Someone was there, holding it. Talking to her in a soothing voice.

Matt? He was saying something about a baby, over and over. 'The baby's all right…he's going to be all right—'

But her baby was—

She felt herself recoil from the pain. It hurt too much to think, to work it all out. She tried to open her eyes, to argue, but it was too bright, too difficult, so she shut them again and let the fog close over her…

'She woke for a moment. She coughed, and she tried to open her eyes.'

'OK, well, that's good. Let's have a look. Amy? Amy, wake up, please, open your eyes. Come on.'

The doctor squeezed her ear, pressing his nail into the lobe, and she moaned slightly but she didn't open her eyes or react in any other way.

He checked her reflexes, scanned the monitor, listened to her chest, checked her notes for urine output and fluid balance, and nodded.

'She's shifting a lot of fluid, which is good. Have you noticed any change?'

'Her hand's thinner.'

He picked it up, pressed it, nodded again, had a look at her incision and covered her, but not before Matt had seen it. He smiled. It was neat. Very neat, for all the hurry. Ben had done a good job. She wouldn't have unsightly scars to trouble her.

'I gather the baby's doing well.'

'Yes, he is. I went to see him. He's beautiful. Amazing. Really strong.'

'Well, she's resting now if you want to go and see him again. I don't think she's about to wake up.'

He nodded. It wasn't what he wanted to hear. He wanted to be told she was lightening, that any minute now she'd drift out of the fog and open her eyes and smile, but he knew it was a vain hope.

Nevertheless, he took the advice and went to see their baby, and as he walked in, he was assailed by fear. He was exhausted, worried sick and for the first time understanding just what all the parents of sick and preterm babies went through.

And it wasn't great.

The shifts had changed, of course, and Rachel wasn't there, but there was another nurse who he'd met before, in September, and she greeted him with a smile. 'Matt, come and see him, he's doing really well. Do you want to hold him?'

He nodded. 'Could I?'

'Of course.' She sat him down, lifted the baby out of the crib and placed him carefully in Matt's arms. Well, hands, really. He was too tiny for arms. With his head in the crook of his arm, his little feet barely reached Matt's wrist, and those skinny, naked feet got to him again. He bent his wrist up and cupped them in his hand, keeping them warm, feeling them flex and wriggle a little as he snuggled them.

He pressed a fingertip to the baby's open palm, and his hand closed, gripping him fiercely. It made him smile. So did the enormous yawn, and then to his delight the baby opened his eyes and stared straight up at him.

'Hello, my gorgeous boy,' he said softly, and then he lost eye contact because his own flooded with a whole range of emotions too huge, too tumultuous to analyse. He sniffed hard, and found a tissue in his hand.

'Thought I might find you here.'

'Are you checking up on me?' he asked gruffly, and Ben dropped into a chair beside him with an understanding smile.

'No, checking up on your son. Daisy wants to see photos, if that's OK?'

'Of course it is. I've been thinking about that. I took one on my phone and sent it to Mum and Dad, but it's not the same.'

'No. I've got my camera, I'll take some and print them. Does he have a name yet, by the way?'

He shook his head. 'I thought you might be able to tell me. I have no idea what Amy was thinking. Not Samuel…' His voice cracked, and he broke off, squeezing his eyes shut and breathing slowly.

Ben squeezed his shoulder, and gave him a moment before going on. 'She'd talked about Joshua—Josh. But

Daisy said she thought Amy was going to ask you about names.'

'She *was* going to tell me about him, then?'

'Oh, God, yes! She said she'd tell you when—'

'What?' he asked, when Ben broke off. 'When what?'

He sighed. 'She said she'd tell you when it was over, one way or the other. That was right at the beginning, when she first found out. She was sixteen weeks pregnant, and I don't think she expected to get this far.'

'I wish you'd been able to tell me.'

'I wish I could have done. I so nearly did, so many times.'

The nurse came back. 'Want to try feeding him? We gave him a bottle an hour ago, and he took a few mils. You could have a go, if you like?'

He took the bottle—a tiny little thing, with not much more than a few spoonfuls in it—and brushed the teat against the baby's cheek. He turned his head towards it, the reflex working perfectly, and Matt slipped the teat between his tiny rosebud lips.

He swallowed reflexively, and then again, and again, and in the end he took most of the small feed while Ben took photos.

How could something so simple be so momentous? The satisfaction was out of all proportion to the task, and Matt grinned victoriously and felt like Superman.

'You need to burp him,' Ben said, pointing the camera at him, and he laughed.

'What, and bring it all up again?'

'That's the way it is. Fairly crazy system but it sort of works.'

Matt shifted the baby so he was against his shoulder, resting on a clean blanket the nurse had draped over him.

'So how's my nephew doing?' he asked as he rubbed the little back gently.

'Really well. He's terrific. Daisy's in her element. Feeding's going really well, and she's feeling stronger by the hour, and it's good.'

'Does he sleep?'

Ben's smile was wry. 'I have no idea what he did last night. I was either here or out for the count. But Daisy was still smiling this morning.'

'That's a good sign.'

The nurse reappeared and asked Ben to have a word with the lady he'd seen in here before, then she turned to him with a smile. 'All gone? Brilliant. Has he burped?'

'Yup.'

'Nappy?'

He laughed quietly. 'I'll give it a go, now my brother's not here taking photos to taunt me with, but don't abandon me. I might stick it on the wrong way up.'

He didn't. He wiped the funny, skinny, wrinkly little bottom dry, got the nappy back onto him without sticking the tabs on his skin or cutting off his circulation or leaving massive gaps, and, feeling ridiculously pleased with himself, he went with Ben to see how Amy was doing.

There was still no change, so after talking to the staff so Ben could catch up on her general progress, they went for a coffee and something to eat, just because he knew he had to keep his strength up, but the moment it was finished he was twitching.

'I need to get back to her,' he said, and draining his coffee, he pushed the chair back and stood up.

'Want company?'

He shook his head. 'Not really. Do you mind? It's

good to touch base and I really appreciate your support, but—I just want to talk to her, say all the things I've never said.'

Ben's hand gripped his shoulder. 'You go for it,' he said softly, and with a gentle smile, he left him to make his own way back. 'I'll bring you the photos. Keep in touch,' he called, turning as he walked away, and Matt nodded.

He would. Just as soon as there was anything to say...

He was there again.

She could hear him talking, his voice soft, wrapping round her and cradling her in a soft cocoon. She couldn't hear the words. Not really, not well enough to make them out, but it was lovely to hear his voice.

She tried to move, and felt a searing pain low down on her abdomen, and she gasped, the blissful cocoon vanishing. It hurt—everything hurt, and someone was holding her, gripping her hands.

'Amy? Amy, it's Matt. It's OK. You're safe, and the baby's safe. He's doing well. It's OK, my darling. You're all right. You're much better and you're going to be OK now.'

She lay still, sifting through the words with her fuddled brain, trying to claw through the fog. Something was wrong. Something...

The baby's safe...he's doing well...

But he wasn't. He wasn't safe at all! Why was Matt telling her that? He knew she'd lost him, he knew that, so why was he lying to her?

She heard a strange noise, like someone crying, a long, long way away, and then the fog closed over her again...

* * *

'She woke up. I was telling her everything was all right, and she started crying, and then she was gone again.'

'Don't worry. She could just be in pain,' the doctor said, and he stepped outside for a minute to stretch his legs and give them room to get to her. God, he needed Ben, but he couldn't ask.

He went back inside. They were nearly finished. They'd topped up her pain relief and checked her thoroughly. She was coming up now, hovering just under the surface of consciousness, and he was feeling sick with dread. This was the time he'd find out just how bad she was, how much brain damage she might have sustained during the fit, or in fact before it, causing it.

A part of him didn't want to know, but the other part, the part that still, incredibly, dared to believe, wanted her to wake.

And then finally, what seemed like hours later, when he was getting desperate, she opened her eyes.

'Amy? Amy, it's Matt.'

His face swam, coming briefly into focus. So it *was* him there with her. She'd thought so. Emotion threatened to choke her, and as if he knew that he leant forwards, gripping her hand.

'How are you feeling?'

'Sore,' she said hoarsely, answering the question because it was easier than thinking about why he was there by her side in hospital. 'My head's sore. And—everywhere, really. Why do I feel like this?'

'You went into pre-eclampsia, and you had a fit,' he told her gently, her hand wrapped firmly in his. 'Ben had to deliver the baby, but he's OK. He's doing really well.'

She shook her head, slowly at first, then more urgently, because he was wrong and she had to tell him. 'No. Ben wasn't there.'

'Yes, he was. He delivered you, Amy. We found you on the floor.'

Yes. She remembered the floor. Remembered crumpling to the floor, someone coming to her, lifting her up, calling Matt. Telling him she was losing the baby…

She closed her eyes against the images, but they followed her, tearing her apart. 'I lost him. I'm sorry…'

'No, Amy.' He was insistent, confusing her. 'Amy, he's fine. He's going to be fine. He's all right.'

'No,' she whispered. 'No. I've lost him. I saw him, Matt! I saw him! Why are you lying to me?' she asked frantically, feeling panic and the raw, awful pain of loss sweeping over her and deluging her with emotion. She brushed his hands away, desperate to be rid of the feel of him, hanging onto her and lying, lying.

'Don't lie to me! He's dead—you know he's dead!'

He had her hands again, his grip inescapable, still lying to her. 'Amy, no! Listen, please listen, you're confused, I'm not lying to you, he's alive.'

'Stop it! Don't lie to me! Stop it!' she screamed, pressing her hands to her ears to block out the sound of his voice, but she could still hear him, over and over again, lying to her, the sound ringing in her head and driving her mad with grief.

'*He's alive…alive…alive…*'

'No-o-o-o—! Go away! I hate you! Leave me alone, don't do this.'

'Shh, Amy, it's all right, hush now, go back to sleep,' a firm, gentle voice told her. 'It's all right. Easy now.'

'Ben?' she whispered, her voice slurring. She struggled to get the words out, but they wouldn't come. 'Ben, he's lying, get him away from me! Get him away.'

'Hush, Amy, it's OK. He's gone. You go to sleep. Everything's all right.'

She wanted to argue, to tell him it wasn't all right. It was really important to tell them, but she felt herself sliding back down, felt the pain slip away as the fog wrapped her again in gentle, mindless oblivion...

Ben caught up with him in the loo off the corridor. The door was hanging open as he'd left it, and he was shaking.

He felt a gentle hand on his back. 'You all right?' Ben asked softly, and Matt straightened and leant back against the wall, shuddering.

'Ben, I can't take it. I can't do this.'

Ben shoved a tissue into his hand. 'Yes, you can. She'll be all right. She's just confused, but it'll pass. It's the sedation and the pressure on her brain from the fluid, not to mention the other drugs, the painkillers, the magnesium sulphate.' Matt lifted a hand to ward off the words, and Ben flushed the loo. 'Wash your face and hands, and come and sit down and talk this through with me. You know what's going on. She's having flashbacks, but she'll come out of it.'

'Will she? I'm not so sure,' he said, and swallowed hard as bile rose in his throat again.

'I'm sure. Come on. Sort yourself out and we'll go for a walk. You could use some fresh air.'

Fresh air? He could think of plenty of things he needed. Fresh air wasn't one of them. What he needed was a miracle, but in the absence of that, his brother's support was the next best thing.

He washed his face and hands, took a long, deep breath and went.

CHAPTER SIX

IT WAS quiet when she woke again.

Quiet, and calm.

Well, calm for the hospital, anyway. There were still the bleeps and tweets and hissings of the machines, the ringing phones in the distance, the sound of hurrying feet, someone talking, but there was a quietness about it.

Night-time, she realised.

She opened her eyes and looked around, slightly stunned. HDU? Wow. She was hooked up to all sorts of things, and Matt was asleep in the chair beside her, his top half slumped on the bottom of the bed, his head resting on one arm and the other hand lying loosely on hers. She couldn't see his face, it was hidden by a fold in the bedcover, but she knew it was him.

She thought he'd been there all the time—had a feeling she'd heard his voice in the distance. Oh. So hard. She blinked to clear her vision, to clear her mind, but it felt like glue.

She tried moving—carefully, just a little, because she was feeling sore. Something momentous had happened, but she couldn't remember what.

Samuel, her mind said, but she knew that was wrong.

Samuel was years ago, and she could feel the sadness for him, the ache that never left her, but stronger now for some reason, and tinged with fear.

She eased her hand away from Matt's and felt her tummy. Soft, flabby—and tender, low down. A—dressing? A post-op dressing?

A section? Why had she had a section? Oh, think! she told herself. There was something there, just hovering out of reach, and she tried again.

Yes. She'd had a headache. It was a dreadful headache. She'd had it all day, getting worse, but when she'd got home it was awful. And then—

'Oh!'

Her soft gasp jerked Matt awake, and he sat up with a grunt, grabbing his neck and rubbing it, his head rotating, easing out the kinks. His smile was tired and—wary? 'Amy. You're awake. Are you OK?'

She nodded. He looked awful. He hadn't shaved, his clothes were crumpled and his eyes were red-rimmed. From exhaustion? Or crying? He'd looked like this before...

'Matt, what happened?' she asked, not sure if she wanted to know the answer. His face...

'You had pre-eclampsia,' he said carefully. 'Do you remember that?'

She nodded slowly, trying to think, trying to suppress the niggle of fear. 'Yes. Sort of. I had a dreadful headache. Were you there? I've got this vague recollection of you carrying me...'

His face crumpled for a moment, so she thought something terrible had happened. He looked so drained, and she felt her heart rate start to pick up. The baby...

'Yes, I was there. I'd come up to see Ben and Daisy's

baby for the weekend. We heard you at the door, and when I opened it you'd collapsed on the floor. That was when I carried you. We brought you to the hospital.'

He waited, and she thought about it. Yes, she remembered that—not the hospital, but before then, his face looming over her, his arms round her, making her feel safe. And Ben and Daisy's baby. Of course. She'd delivered Thomas—when? Recently. Very recently. But—

'I had a section,' she said, not daring to ask and yet she could hear his voice in her head, saying he was all right, it was OK, the baby was fine. But there was something else, about him lying to her, some little niggle...

He smiled, his eyes lighting with a tender joy. 'Yes. We had a boy, Amy,' he told her, his voice shaking slightly. 'He's fine. He's a little small, but he's doing really well, he's a proper fighter. Ben took some photos for you.'

He held them out to her, and she saw a baby almost lost in Matt's arms. There was a clip on his finger, and leads trailing from his tiny chest, and the nappy seemed to drown him, but he looked pink and well and—alive?

She sucked in a breath, and then another, hardly daring to believe it as the hope turned to joy. 'Is he—is that really...?'

'It's our baby, Amy,' he said softly, his eyes bright. 'He's in SCBU and he's doing really well.'

He showed her another photo, a close-up just of the baby, and she traced the features with her finger, wondering at them. Amazing. So, so amazing...

'Can I see him? I want to see him. Can you take me?'

He shook his head. 'You can't leave the ward yet, sweetheart. You're still on the magnesium sulphate infusion, and you've been really ill.'

'I want to see him. I want to hold him,' she said, and she started to cry, because she'd been so afraid for so long, and there was still something there, something lurking in the fringes of the fog behind her, something terrifying that she didn't understand. 'Please let me hold him.'

'OK, OK, sweetheart, don't cry, I'll go and get him. I'll bring him to you.' She felt him gather her up in his arms, his face next to hers, the stubble rough and oddly reassuring against her cheek. 'Hush now,' he murmured gently. 'Come on, lie back and rest. It's all right. Just relax—'

His voice cracked, and she wanted to cry again, but for him this time. He'd had no warning of this. She'd been going to tell him, to explain, but she'd run out of time, and for him to find her like that—

'It's OK, Matt, I'm all right,' she said, reassuring him hastily. 'I'm fine. Please, just bring him to me. Let me see him. I need to see him with my own eyes. I need to know he's all right.'

'He's all right, I promise you, Amy, and I'm not lying. I'll get him—give me five minutes. I'll get someone to come and see you while I fetch him.'

He hesitated, then carefully, as if he was afraid to hurt her, he lifted her hand to his lips and pressed a gentle kiss to her palm, then folded her fingers over it to keep it safe while he was gone.

Her eyes flooded with tears. He'd always done that, right since their first date. The last time he'd done it was after Samuel died...

'Amy, it's good to see you awake. How are you?'

She blinked away the tears and smiled up at the nurse who was both friend and colleague in another life. 'I don't know, Kate. OK, I think. My head hurts, and my tummy's sore, but—Matt's gone to get the baby...?' she said, ending it almost as a question, but Kate smiled widely.

'Yes, he has. We can't let you off the ward yet, not till your magnesium sulphate infusion's finished, but he can come to you for a little while. You'll feel so much better when you've had a cuddle. Let's get you a little wash and sit you up. You'll feel better when you've cleaned your teeth, too.'

She'd feel better when she'd seen her baby, Amy thought, but she let Kate help her up, let her wash her and comb her hair, and she cleaned her teeth—Kate was right, it did feel better when her teeth were clean—and then she was ready, her heart pounding, every second an hour as she waited to hold her little son for the first time.

'He's gorgeous,' Kate said, smiling and tidying up. 'Ben's been in flashing photos of both of them, and he's just like their baby. Smaller, of course, but lovely. So cute. Oh, look, here he comes, the little man!'

Matt was trundling the clear plastic crib, and Amy scooted up the bed a bit more, Kate helping her and tutting and rearranging her pillows, and with a crooked smile Matt lifted his tiny, precious cargo out of the crib and laid him in her waiting arms.

Gosh, he was so small! He weighed next to nothing, his feet hardly reaching her hand, his little head perfectly round, but he was breathing, his chest moving, one arm flailing in his sleep.

She lifted him to her face, kissed him, inhaled the scent of his skin and felt calm steal over her. This was her child, here in her arms where he belonged, alive and well and safe. The last cobwebs of her nightmare were torn aside as she looked at him, taking in each feature, watching his little mouth working, his eyelids flicker as he screwed up his button nose, and she laughed softly in delight.

'He's so tiny!' she breathed, staring down at him in wonder. She took his hand, and the fingers closed on her thumb, bringing a huge lump to her throat, but then his eyes opened and locked with hers, and she felt everything right itself, the agonising suspense of the last six months wiped out in a moment. 'Hello, baby,' she said softly, her voice rising naturally to a pitch he could hear. 'Oh, aren't you so beautiful? My gorgeous, gorgeous boy...'

'He's due a feed,' Matt said softly, after a moment. 'They've given me a bottle for you to give him, if you want to.'

She felt shocked. 'A bottle?'

'Of breast milk, from the bank. Just until you're well enough, and because he's suffered a setback with the pre-eclampsia, so he needs to catch up. But if you want to try...'

She did. She desperately wanted to feel him against her skin, to touch him, nurse him, hold him.

They pulled the screens round her, and Kate eased the gown off her shoulders and then put the baby back into her arms. He was only wearing a nappy, and she felt his skin against her breasts, so soft, so thin it was almost transparent.

'He's too sleepy.'

'No, he's not. His mouth's working, look. He'll wake up if you stroke your nipple against his cheek.'

Oh, genius child! He knew exactly what to do. She

touched his soft, delicate cheek with her nipple, and he turned his head, rosebud lips open, and as she'd done countless times with other mothers, she pressed the baby's head against the breast and he latched on. And just like that, he was suckling.

Relief poured through her, because so often if babies suffered a setback at this stage and had to be bottle fed for the first days or weeks, it could become almost impossible to establish breast feeding. Not so with her baby, she thought with a flurry of maternal pride.

'He's amazing,' she said contentedly. 'So clever.'

'He is,' Matt agreed, tucking a blanket gently round them to keep him warm. 'He's incredible. So are you.' He stared down at them both, at the little jaws working hard, the milk-beaded lips around her nipple, her finger firmly held by the tiny hand of this miracle that was their child.

It had taken them twenty-seven hours, but finally, mother and son were getting acquainted, her crisis had passed and they could look to the future—a brighter future than he'd dared to imagine.

Where it would take them, though, he still had no idea…

Amy didn't quite know what to do with Matt.

He'd taken the baby back to the neonatal unit after she'd finished feeding him, and once he'd changed his nappy and he was settled, he came back to see her.

She was lying down again, exhausted with emotion and effort, and the first thing he did was stick up the photos of the baby on the side of her locker right in front of her, so she could see them.

'OK now?' he asked gently, and she nodded tiredly.

'I'm fine. Bit sore. I could do with going to sleep, and you look as if you could, too. Why don't you go back to Ben and Daisy's and get your head down? Or mine,' she added, and then wondered if that was really such a good idea, but he latched onto it instantly.

'That might be better. They're getting little enough sleep as it is. I think Thomas has his own idea of a schedule and I don't think night-time features yet.'

She smiled at that. 'Babies don't do schedules—well, not at three days old or whatever he is now.'

'Day three today, which started about half an hour ago. It's just after midnight on Sunday. You had the baby on Friday night.'

She frowned. 'So long ago? How long was I out?'

'A long time. Over twenty-four hours.'

She reached out her hand, and he took it, his fingers wrapping firmly round hers and squeezing gently. 'That must have been awful for you,' she murmured, and his mouth twitched into a fleeting smile.

'I don't think you were enjoying it much either.'

She frowned again. 'No.'

'You're OK now, and so's he. And you're right, I could do with getting my head down. It's been a tough week at work and I haven't had any sleep to speak of since Thursday morning.'

He got to his feet, and hesitated. 'Are you sure you're all right if I leave you?'

'Absolutely sure,' she promised, really tired now. 'I need to sleep, too. My head's killing me.'

'It'll be better soon. Give it another few hours. You sleep well, and I'll see you in the morning. Get them to call my mobile if there's anything you want—anything at all.'

And as if he knew the only thing she really wanted was a hug, he leant over and gave her one, a gentle squeeze as his stubble brushed her cheek and he dropped a feather-light kiss on the corner of her mouth.

'Sleep tight,' he murmured, and kissing her hand again, he folded up her fingers and left her alone with her thoughts.

When he got back to the hospital in the morning, it was to find that Amy had been moved out of HDU into a single room on the postnatal ward, and he went to find her.

'Hi there,' he said, tapping on the door and pushing it open with a smile. 'How are you?'

'Much better. My hands and feet feel as if they might be mine again, and my headache's easing.' She frowned, and tipped her head on one side, eyeing him searchingly. 'Just how bad was it, Matt? Nobody seems to want to tell me and the consultant's not around, conveniently.'

'No. Well, I think Ben's sort of overseeing your care.'

'You mean you aren't?' she asked, only half joking.

Curiously, he hadn't felt the need to interfere, and he told her so. 'I think it's because I was keeping a pretty close eye on what was going on, and they were doing what I would have done, so there was no need.'

'You haven't answered the first question,' she pointed out, and he grunted softly and sat down on the chair beside her.

'You—uh—you fitted. In HDU, after the delivery.'

Amy was stunned. 'I fitted?' she said, thinking that it explained a lot about her headache. 'So what was my blood pressure?'

'At its highest? It went up to 240 over 180.'

She felt her jaw drop, and she shut her mouth and swallowed. Hard. 'Wow.'

'Do you know what it is now?'

She shook her head, and he checked on the chart in the rack by the door. 'One-sixty over 80. Still high, but coming down well. What's your baseline?'

'One-twenty over 70. I can't believe that. That's shocking!'

'Yes. It wasn't great,' he said drily.

'Were you there?'

He nodded. 'I was, pretty much all the time. Ben dragged me away for a few minutes a couple of times in the first twenty-four hours, but mostly I was there, and—well, it wasn't great spectator sport, let's put it like that. I'd rather be on the other side organising the treatment any day.'

She looked down, fiddling with the edge of the sheet. 'There's something I can't— Did we have a row? It's really foggy, I'm not sure if I dreamed it or what, but— did I accuse you of lying to me?'

His eyebrows scrunched up slightly, and he gave a reluctant nod. 'Yes. Yes, you did, but—'

'About the baby?'

'You were drugged up to the eyeballs, Amy. You didn't know what was going on.'

'I thought he was dead, didn't I?' she said slowly, sifting through the snippets of memory lurking in the fog, and then she looked up and met his eyes. 'I thought it was—last time,' she said softly. 'Didn't I?'

He nodded slowly, his eyes pained. 'Yes. You muddled them up, and thought I was lying when I said he was all right.'

Her eyes filled with tears, and she looked away. 'It

still seems wrong that this baby's OK and—' She broke off, then carried on, 'We need a name for him. We can't just keep calling him the baby.'

'Daisy said you liked Joshua.'

'I do, but I wanted to ask you. He's your baby, too. Do you like it?'

'It's fine—yes, I do. It's a good name.' He hesitated, not sure how to say this, how it would land. 'I thought— maybe we could call him Joshua Samuel.'

Her breath caught on a tiny sob. 'That's lovely,' she said, and biting her lip, she turned away.

Joshua Samuel. Both her boys.

Oh, lord.

She started to cry, broken, hiccupping little sobs, and found herself cradled tenderly against a broad, firm chest. 'I miss him,' she wept, and she felt him tense under her hands.

'I know, sweetheart, I know,' he murmured gruffly. 'I miss him, too.'

'Why did he have to die?' she asked, sniffing back the tears and pulling away. Her hands scrubbed at her face, swiping the tears aside, but fresh ones took their place and he reached for a tissue and handed it to her.

'I don't know. We'll never know. There didn't seem to be anything wrong with him, or you. It was just one of those things.'

'We went for a walk—the day before. A long one.'

'Yes. We did. But we often walked, Amy. It was what we did. We walked miles all the time, so it was nothing new. And you know that. You can't blame yourself, it wasn't your fault, or anything you or anybody else did. I braked sharply in the car on the way home, on the motorway. It could have been that, but it's unlikely. It was just one of those unexplained tragedies that happen in obstetrics. You know we don't have the answer to all of them. Sometimes things just happen.'

She nodded, and looked up at the clock on the wall. 'I need to feed him. They said if he's gained weight, I can have him with me here, and then we can go home together in a few days. They're really pleased with him.'

'Good.' His smile was wry. 'I'm really pleased with him, too. I would have liked to have been here with you, to have known you were pregnant, to have shared it.'

She swallowed the guilt. It was too late to do anything about it, but even if she could, she wouldn't have told him until after 26 weeks, at least. 'I'm sorry. I just—'

'Couldn't let yourself believe it would be all right?'

Her smile was sad. 'Something like that,' she admitted.

'So what do we do now, Amy?' he asked, his voice soft. 'What happens next?'

The real question was too hard to answer, so she didn't even try.

'Now, we feed the baby,' she said, and started the slow and uncomfortable process of getting out of bed.

She had a rest later, and Ben came in and they went outside in the grounds with a coffee.

'So what happens now?' Ben asked quietly, echoing his own words to Amy, and Matt felt himself frown.

'I don't know. It all depends on Amy, on what she feels about my involvement.'

'Are you taking paternity leave?'

He gave a short huff of laughter. 'I have no idea. I haven't really had time to consider it. It's not a good time at work, but then it never is, is it? I've got some

twins I don't really want to delegate—I need to be backwards and forwards. But if Amy will let me, I want to
be around, and I'm certainly going to be part of his life.'

'I didn't doubt it for a moment,' Ben said drily. 'I just
wonder if Amy's thought it through, or if she never let
herself get that far. She hasn't bought any baby equip-
ment according to Daisy. Not so much as a nappy.'

He frowned again. She really had been blanking it
out. He wondered why. Was it simply because she didn't
think it would be all right? Or was it because she'd never
really grieved for Samuel and hadn't moved on? Their
relationship had fallen apart so soon after she lost him
that Matt had no idea how she'd dealt with it. Now, he
was beginning to wonder if she'd dealt with it at all.

He wasn't sure how well he'd dealt with it—not well
at the time, certainly, and the thought of his first son
left a hollow ache in his chest even now. But this was
Joshua's time, he told himself firmly, and wondered how
much of him he'd see, in reality.

Should he take paternity leave? Instinct said yes, but
Amy might have other ideas. He'd talk to her about it,
but he'd certainly investigate the possibility.

They kept her in for the rest of the week, and it felt like
the busiest week of his life.

He had twins he was monitoring at the unit in
London, and his specialist registrar called on Monday
night to say they were concerned, so he drove down,
weighed up all the results, added in his gut feeling and
delivered them at four in the morning, then went into
his office and cleared his outstanding paperwork. By
the time HR were in at nine, he'd delegated responsibility for his cases, divvied them out according to se-

verity, written a short—very short—list of patients he insisted on seeing himself, and was ready to go back.

The time he'd been away had enabled him to make one decision, at least. He phoned HR, told them he was taking paternity leave, notified them of the cover arrangements he'd put in place, and after a short detour to his house to pack some things, he was back in Suffolk by Amy's side before lunch.

'Gosh, you look tired.'

He laughed softly. 'Yeah. Been a bit busy. Some twins decided they'd had enough.'

'In London?'

He nodded. 'They were only twenty-seven weeks, but they were already struggling and they hadn't grown for five days. They're OK, but they were tiny.'

'They would be,' she said softly. 'Heavens. And I'm worried about our Josh.'

'Are you?' he asked instantly, and she shook her head.

'No. Not any more. Sorry, that was a bad choice of words. It's just that I mostly deliver babies that are term, and anything as small as those twins must be...'

Brings back Samuel, he thought, understanding instantly, and he wondered how she did her job, how she coped with stillbirths and labours so early that the babies couldn't be viable. By blanking it out? Well, it worked for him. More or less.

'How's the feeding going?' he asked, sticking to a safe topic, and her face softened into a smile.

'Great. He's doing really well. I think they're going to say we can go home in a day or two.' The smile faded, and she bit her lip.

'What?' he said quietly.

'I've been a bit silly,' she admitted. It was easy to say

it, now he was all right, but before—well it had been hard to plan ahead. 'I haven't bought anything for him. No clothes, nappies, cot—nothing. I was going to do it as soon as I started maternity leave.' If she'd got that far. Well, she certainly had now, she thought wryly. 'I wonder how long things take to come if you order them over the internet. Sometimes it's quite quick.'

'Or you could write me a list. I'll just get the basic stuff in ready for you to bring him home, and you can have all the fun of the cute, pretty stuff with Daisy once you're a bit stronger.'

It was so tempting. Just hand it all over to him and sit back and concentrate on Joshua. Which of course was what she should be doing, she realised. 'Would you mind? And it really needn't be a lot. I'll move some money into your bank account—'

'I hardly think it's necessary for you to refund me for basic purchases I make for my own child,' he said with that quiet implacability she was beginning to re-alise she couldn't argue with. Well, not and win, any-way. Pointless trying, so she vowed to keep the list as short as possible and do the bulk of the shopping once he'd gone back. He couldn't take much longer off work, surely?

'Incidentally, I'm on paternity leave,' he told her, as if he'd read her mind. 'Except for a few days here and there. I still need to go back a couple of days a week and I'm on standby for emergencies in my trickier cases, but otherwise I'll be here, giving you a hand until you're back on your feet.'

He wasn't asking, she noticed, and she wondered if she ought to mind, but in fact it was a relief. She'd been dreading going home, having to cope alone or, her reluctant alternative in an emergency, troubling Ben and Daisy.

She was sure they wouldn't mind. They'd been brilliant. Daisy had been in twice, Ben was always popping in because, like Matt, there were cases he didn't feel he could hand over, but they had their own new baby to worry about, and she didn't want to get in the way of that joyful time.

And now, she wouldn't have to, because she'd have the baby's father there staking his claim—

No! Stop it! Of course he has rights, and you want him to be there for your baby!

'If you're sure you can spare the time, that would be really helpful for a few days,' she said.

A few days.

He'd had in mind a lifetime, but after the road they'd travelled in the last four years, he'd settle for a few days as an opener.

'Let's write your list,' he said, pulling out his phone. It doubled as a notebook, so he keyed in the items as she thought of them, and when she was done he closed it and put it back in his pocket.

'I think it's time for a cuddle,' he said, standing up and peeling back the little blanket carefully, and sliding his hands under him he picked Joshua up without disturbing him at all.

She watched him, loving the sure, confident way he handled his son, knowing he was safe. She'd always loved watching him with babies. When she'd first worked with him, six years ago, she'd known he'd be good with his own. That had been one of the hardest things about losing Samuel—watching Matt holding him, the gentleness of his hands as he'd cradled the much-too-tiny baby, kissed him, before laying him tenderly on the white cloth, covering him…

She'd never seen him cry for Samuel, but she'd heard him. She'd envied him, because she hadn't been able to, not then, not for a long time.

But now—now he was holding Joshua, and his hands were just as gentle, just as sure, and the love in his eyes was just as certain.

If only he loved her. If only she could trust that love.

No. She wanted him in Josh's life, and she could trust him with her son without a doubt. She just wasn't sure she could trust him with herself.

CHAPTER SEVEN

HE WENT back to see her that evening, and found several of her colleagues standing around her, laughing and talking.

The moment he walked in, however, they stopped dead, smiled at him and left. 'Don't mind me,' he said, holding up his hands, but they went anyway, and he shook his head, slightly bemused, and sat down next to Amy.

'Was it something I said?'

'No, of course not. They're just—they don't really know what to say to you.'

'Hello would be a good start,' he said drily, and she chuckled, but then she pulled a face.

'One of the advantages of giving birth in your workplace is that you get spoilt to bits, but the disadvantage is that they think of you as public property, and there's only been one question on all their minds since they realised I was pregnant, and they've just found out the answer's you. That's why they can't talk to you. I think they feel a bit awkward, with you being Ben's brother.'

He was puzzled. 'Didn't they know I was the father?'

'No, of course not. I hadn't said anything about you, and I actively discouraged curious questions, but I suppose now I'm on the mend, and the baby's all right, they've stopped worrying about us and I can just *hear* the cogs turning. You know what hospitals are like.'

'You don't think they'd worked it out before?'

She shrugged. 'Maybe. Several of them were there for the evening do at the wedding, so it's quite possible someone saw us together and worked it out. Nobody really seems surprised, I guess.'

'No. I imagine they just want to know all the gory details.'

'Well, they aren't getting them from me,' she said firmly. 'I hate being the object of curiosity.'

'Yeah, me too. How's Josh?'

'OK. He's under the UV light. I thought he was looking a bit jaundiced when I changed his nappy, so they called the paediatrician. I thought they would have told you.'

'They did. It's quite common, nothing to worry about.'

He didn't know why he was reassuring her, except that she looked a little glum, and she tried to smile.

'I know that,' she said. 'It just seems odd without him here.'

'It's not for long.'

'I know.'

He frowned. There was something in her voice, something that didn't feel quite right, and he got up and went over to her, perching on the edge of the bed and looking down at her searchingly.

'Hey, what's up?' he asked softly, brushing her cheek with his knuckles, and just like that tears slid down her cheek.

'Oh, Amy,' he murmured, and easing her into his

arms, he cradled her against his shoulder and rocked her gently. 'What's up, sweetheart? Are you worried about him? You don't need to be.'

She shook her head. 'No. I just miss him being here. It scares me,' she said, hiccupping on a sob. 'I don't like it when I can't see him, and I need to feed him, and my milk's come in and I feel as if I've got rocks on my chest and everything hurts—'

She broke off, sobbing in earnest now, and he shushed her gently and smoothed her hair.

'You've got the four-day blues, ' he said tenderly. 'All those hormones sloshing around. It'll soon pass. Do you want to go down there and feed him?'

She sniffed and nodded, and he got off the bed and handed her a hot, wrung-out face flannel to wipe away her tears, and then he helped her out of bed and walked her down to the neonatal unit. She was steady on her feet now, but he walked with his arm round her—just in case there was anyone there left in any doubt that he was Josh's father and definitely in the picture—and he handed Josh to her and sat beside her while she was feeding him.

'Ow, they're too full, it hurts,' she said, her eyes welling again, and he gave her another hug.

'It'll soon be easier. Give it a minute and you'll be fine, and it'll get better. You'd rather it was this way than you didn't have enough.'

'Do you have to be right about everything?' she sniped tearfully, and he blew out his breath slowly and took his arm away.

'Sorry. I was only trying to help.'

'Well, don't. I know all that. I don't need to be told—'

She broke off, knowing full well she was being un-reasonable, but...

'Do you want me to go home?' he asked quietly, and she thought, *Home? As in your home, in London, or my home?* The answer was the same, whatever. She shook her head.

'No. I'm sorry, I'm just tired,' she said. 'Tired and fed up and I want to go home myself.'

He gave a short sigh and put his arm round her again. To hell with it. She needed comforting, and he was right here, and the person who arguably should be doing it. Who else, for heaven's sake?

'You can come home soon,' he murmured soothingly. 'You could come home tonight, if you wanted. You're well enough. It's only the feeding, and you could spend the days here and stay at home for the nights. You could express the milk—'

She shook her head. 'I can't leave him, Matt. I can't leave my baby all night. I can't...'

Poor Amy. She'd been on an emotional rollercoaster for the last few months, and it wasn't over yet, he knew. They had so many unresolved issues, and if nothing else, they had to build a working relationship for the future.

'Stay, then, but I think you should restrict your visitors. They're wearing you out.'

She sighed and leant into him, her head finding its natural resting place on his shoulder. 'But they're lovely to me,' she said wearily. 'They've brought all sorts of presents, and they make me laugh and they're so kind, really.'

'I know they are, but you're tired, Amy. You need some rest. Come on, let me take him and deal with him now, and you go back to bed and get some rest.'

She nodded, and he took Josh, resting him against his shoulder where Amy's head had just been. He was getting good at winding him—he'd been practising on Thomas in between times, and he'd got it down to a fine art now.

He put him back under the UV light with his eye-shade on, changed his nappy and left him to sleep. He fussed for a moment and then settled, and Matt went back to Amy and found her curled on her side in the bed, clutching a handful of tissues and sniffing.

'Can I have a cuddle?' she asked tearfully, so he tipped the blinds in the door, turned down the lights and lay down beside her, easing her into his arms.

'You've really been through the mill, haven't you?' he murmured, holding her close, and she sniffed again and burrowed closer. 'It's OK, I've got you. You're all right,' he said softly, and gradually the little shuddering sobs died away, and he felt her body relax, her breathing slowing as she slid into sleep.

He stayed there for an hour, until there was a quiet tap on the door and it opened to reveal Rachel, the nurse from SCBU.

'How is she?'

'Asleep,' he mouthed. 'Problem?'

'He's brought up his feed and he's hungry again. Shall I bring him to her, just for a minute? Don't move her. She's been a bit weepy today. I think she missed you while you were away.'

Had she? He woke her gently. 'Sweetheart, the baby needs feeding again, but you don't have to move. Rachel's bringing him.'

She made a sleepy little sound of protest, opened her

eyes and breathed in shakily. 'Oh, I'm so tired, Matt. I can't do this.'

'Yes, you can. Just feed him. All you have to do is sit there. We'll do the rest.'

She let him help her up against the pillows, and stared at him searchingly. 'Why are you doing all of this for me?' she asked, sounding genuinely perplexed, and he gave a soft laugh.

'Because I love you—both of you,' he replied, as if it was obvious, and then Rachel came in and there wasn't time to say any more.

But it stayed with her all night, the words keeping her company every time she woke to feed the baby or go to the loo or just to turn over, and although she wasn't sure if she could trust them, still they comforted her.

It might be true, she thought. Or at least, if he hung around long enough, maybe it would become true. People did learn to love each other, given time.

One day at a time, she told herself, just as she had through her pregnancy. One day at a time...

She went home with Joshua two days later.

Her blood pressure was much closer to normal, her hands and feet and face were her own again, and his jaundice had cleared up, so they were to be allowed out, and it couldn't come soon enough for her.

Matt came to fetch her, armed with a couple of bags. He was a few minutes late, but he'd been busy, he said. On the phone, probably, she thought, sorting out one of his cases in London, but he produced some clothes for her and the baby.

'They'll probably drown him,' he said, 'but they were supposed to be for babies of his weight.'

He looked out of his depth—strangely, for a man so at home with babies, but they were usually either still tucked up inside their mothers or slippery and screaming when he handled them, so all things considered he was doing well, and she smiled at him.

'I'm sure they'll be fine. Better too big than too small.'

'They won't be too small,' he assured her.

They weren't. She had to turn back the cuffs, and when he bent his legs his little feet disappeared, but he'd soon grow out of the first size. They always did.

'He looks really cute,' she said, smiling at Josh. 'Don't you, my gorgeous?'

The baby stared at her with startlingly blue eyes, so thoughtful.

'I wonder what he makes of us?' Matt said softly.

'I don't know. I wonder if he knows I'm his mother?'

'Of course he does. He'll know your voice.'

It was a lovely thought. She'd said as much to many mums over the years, but this time it was her baby, and she was the mother, and the thought was curiously centring.

'Right, all set?'

She nodded. 'I've packed my things—oh, Matt, we'll need a car seat! I didn't even think of it!'

'All done,' he said calmly. 'It's in the car.'

She had a committee to see her off. 'Isn't anybody in labour?' she asked wryly, as one by one they all hugged her and said goodbye.

'Go on, off you go, and keep in touch,' said Rosie, one of the midwives, hugging her again, and Matt closed the car door, got into the front and drove her home.

Bliss, she thought as he pulled up in the car port at

the back and helped her out. She could sit in the garden and listen to the birds, and spend time in the conservatory soaking up the sun with Josh at her side.

They went through the conservatory into the kitchen, and she walked slowly in and looked around. In the middle of the dining table was a huge bunch of flowers in a tall vase, and they stopped her in her tracks.

'Oh, they're lovely! Who are they from?'

He put the baby seat and her bags down on the floor and gave her a wry smile. 'Me—just to welcome you home.'

'Oh, Matt—thank you. Thank you for everything...'

She hugged him, letting her head rest against his chest for a few moments, but it wasn't fair to hold him at arm's length for months and then lean on him when it suited her, so she straightened up and moved away, walking slowly through her house, touching it as if she was making sure it was still here, grounding herself.

'I bought a few things for the baby,' he said. 'They're upstairs.'

She made her way up there, and found Matt had made himself thoroughly at home.

She'd seen his laptop in the sitting room as she'd put her head in, and his wash things were in the bathroom, set out neatly on the window sill above the basin, and he'd taken over the back bedroom.

He obviously meant what he'd said about being around for her, she realised, and the implications of sharing her house with him, even in the short term, began to dawn on her.

She went into her bedroom, and found he'd changed the sheets on her bed—or someone had. Daisy? Surely not, so soon after having Thomas, but maybe she'd just suggested it and supervised. Daisy had got good at supervising towards the end of her pregnancy, she thought with a smile.

Whatever, it meant she was coming home to clean, crisp linen on the bed, and she had a sudden longing to climb into it and sleep for hours.

And then she looked beyond the bed, and spotted the pretty Moses basket draped with white embroidered cotton by the far side.

'Oh, Matt!' She trailed her fingers lightly over it, and her eyes filled. 'This is lovely—really pretty. Thank you. And all these clothes!' She stared at the little pile of baby clothes and accessories on the chest of drawers, touching them as if she didn't quite believe they were real. She'd put it off for so long, been so afraid to take this pregnancy for granted, and he'd just calmly come in right at the end and picked up all the pieces. He didn't need to do that, and she'd had no right to ask...

She felt a tear spill over and trickle down her cheek, and she brushed it away. 'Thank you so much.'

'Don't be silly, it's nothing. I didn't get many clothes. I didn't want to overdo it and you're bound to be deluged with presents, so they're only the basic vests and sleep suits and things to start him off, but he'll have grown out of them in five minutes anyway.'

She nodded. She had already been given some clothes, cute little things for him to grow into, and she knew he was right. 'They're just perfect. Thank you, you haven't overdone it at all, it's just what I would have got if I'd been a bit more proactive.'

He gave her a wry smile. 'I can quite see why you weren't, it's a bit overwhelming in there, isn't it? And as for the pram business,' he went on, rolling his eyes,

'I spent an hour in there being given a guided tour of how they fold and what clips on what and how they come apart and turn round and zip together, and some have pram inserts and car seats and face this way or that—by the time she'd finished I was utterly confused, so I just bought a seat and a base to put in my car for today, and whatever else you want you'll have to sort out yourself because frankly I think it's going to be down to personal choice and what you need it for, and I have *no* idea where you would even start!'

She bit her lip, picturing him in a sea of dismantled pushchairs, and she just wanted to hug him. Or laugh.

She ended up doing both, and he wrapped his arms round her and hugged her back, and for a moment they just stood there in each other's arms and held each other.

She could have stayed there forever, but that really wasn't wise or practical, so she let him go and stepped back, before she got too used to it, and looked at the Moses basket again.

'This is so pretty.'

'It won't last long, he'll outgrow it in a few months. I nearly got a crib, but I thought you could carry this downstairs and put him out in the garden in it, or in the conservatory, or in the sitting room in the evening, even take him round to see Daisy—it seemed to have all sorts of possibilities that the crib just didn't, and it doesn't stop you having a crib later, or even now if you wanted to. You could just use it downstairs. And, yeah, I thought it looked the part,' he added with a wry grin.

His talk of taking it downstairs held huge appeal. 'Can we take it downstairs and put him in it now? It's such a lovely day, and I've really missed the sunshine, being trapped in the hospital. It would be lovely to sit in the conservatory with the doors open and just enjoy the fresh air, really.'

'Sure. It's easy.' He looked pleased, as if he was glad his idea had met with her approval, and he lifted the basket, folded the stand and carried them both down.

She followed him more slowly, still a little tender, and by the time she'd taken Joshua out of the car seat and followed Matt through to the conservatory he was setting it up.

'Here, out of the sun?' he asked, and she nodded.

'That's lovely. Thank you.'

She laid the baby in it, and he stretched and yawned, his little arms flopped up by his head, the hat askew. 'He looks pretty chilled,' she said with a smile, and Matt laughed.

'Daddy's boy,' he said with a ridiculously proud grin. 'I always used to lie like that, if the photos can be believed. Cup of tea?'

'Oh, that would be brilliant.' She sat down on the chair carefully, her stitches pulling a little, and watched her baby sleeping. It was turning into her favourite occupation, she thought with a smile.

'Better now?'

He was lounging in the doorway, arms folded, one leg crossed over the other, looking utterly at home, and she realised it would be only too easy to get used to having him around.

'So much better,' she said, her words heartfelt. 'Matt, I'm so grateful to you for all you've done this last week. You just dropped everything, and I never expected you to—

'You didn't offer me the chance to discuss what I wanted to do, what role I wanted in your lives,' he pointed out gently, trying to keep the simmering anger under control. Now wasn't the time. 'I would have been here for you all along, Amy, if you'd given me the chance, but you always did like to go it alone.'

She looked down at her hands. 'Not really. I just didn't know how to deal with it—after the night of Ben and Daisy's wedding it all seemed so complicated.'

Oh, yes. He was with her on that. 'I wish I'd known. I would never have left you alone to cope, and you shouldn't have allowed me to.'

'You didn't leave me alone to cope, I sent you away.'

He gave a wry laugh. 'Yeah, you're good at that, aren't you?'

She frowned at him, puzzled. 'What do you mean?'

'When you were ill—out of it, really, and you thought it was Samuel, not Josh—you told me to go away then.'

She bit her lip; her memories of that time were so patchy and veiled in layers of what seemed like fog, but through it all she knew he'd been there, and she wasn't sure she could have coped without him.

'I didn't mean it. I was so confused. I'm glad you didn't, I didn't really want you to go.'

'Didn't you? It sounded like it. You sounded desperate, Amy. And I've heard you saying it before, don't forget, when things were about as bad as they could be. I left you alone then, too, and I shouldn't have done.'

She swallowed. 'I didn't mean it then, either. Not really, not in that way. I just couldn't cope with your grief as well as mine, and the thought of a wedding so soon after we'd lost him—I just couldn't handle it. How could we have a party then, Matt? It felt so wrong. And if we'd known each other well enough, if we'd really known each other, we could have dealt with it, but we didn't, we retreated into our grief and took the easy way out.'

'Easy?'

She tried to smile. 'No, not easy. Nothing about it was easy, but it was easier than talking to a stranger about something I couldn't even bring myself to think about. And you were a stranger, relatively. We'd only worked in the same department for less than a year before I got pregnant, and we were hardly ever on the same shift or working together because I was on the midwifery-led unit and you were in the high risk unit. We hardly ever met up at work, and because we were working shifts we didn't always see each other at night, either, so even when we were living together we were like ships in the night. It was no wonder we struggled to communicate when we were grieving.'

It was true, he thought. They'd thought they'd known each other, they'd certainly wanted each other and talked about getting married, but they *had* been relative strangers, and yet they'd been expected to cope with the loss of their baby. No wonder it had all fallen apart for them. But now...

'Can we start again?' he said quietly, and she looked up at him, propping up the doorframe and looking rugged and kind and troubled, and she felt a flicker of apprehension.

If she said yes, if she let him back into her life, she'd run the risk of losing him again.

And if she didn't, she realised, she'd lose him now.

She took a deep breath.

'We can try,' she said carefully, and something flared in his eyes, something he quickly banked. 'I'm sorry I didn't tell you I was pregnant, but I was so afraid things would go wrong again.'

'Yeah. Ben said you had no confidence in your pregnancy.'

'Would you have done, in my shoes?'

He smiled wryly. 'Probably not. In my own shoes, had I known, had you told me, I like to think I'd have been rational about it.'

'Are you saying I was irrational?' she asked with an edge to her voice, and he sighed and crouched down beside her.

'No, Amy, I'm not saying that at all. Your reaction was perfectly natural and understandable, but maybe if I'd been with you I could have helped to reassure you.'

'And if it had happened again? If we'd lost Josh?'

His eyes flicked to the baby, and a spasm of pain showed on his face.

'No. I didn't think so. We didn't cope with this before, Matt, and there was nothing to suggest we'd cope with it any better a second time.'

He nodded. 'I'm sorry. I'm not very good at sharing my feelings.'

She laughed at that, a sad little hiccup of laughter that twisted his heart, and he straightened up and moved away, giving them both space. This wasn't going to be as easy as he'd imagined, he realised. No dropping seamlessly back into their old relationship, as if they'd just cut out the last five years and joined the ends together.

'About the next few weeks,' he said, getting back to practicalities because it was far easier than pursuing the other topic. 'I don't want to overcrowd you, and I don't want you to feel abandoned, either. I have to go back to London on Monday for a couple of days, and then I'll be back, and we can see how it goes. I'll try and give you space, and help with Joshua, and if it all gets too much you can kick me out and I can go and see Ben and Daisy and Thomas, or I can go back to London for the night and give you room. We'll play it by ear. Deal?'

She searched his eyes, and found only sincerity and a genuine desire to make this work. The rest could wait.

'Deal,' she said, and she smiled. 'Can we have that tea now? I'm parched.'

Ben and Daisy came round a little later, bearing plates of food and bottles of sparkling water.

'Just because we ought to have something fizzy to wet the babies' heads, and half of us can't drink,' Daisy explained, hugging Amy and bending over Josh and making besotted noises.

'He's so tiny! He's like a mini-Thomas! Oh, I want a cuddle. Hurry up and wake up!'

'No! He's only just gone back to sleep!' Amy said sternly. 'You leave him alone this minute and come and tell me all about Thomas. I feel dreadful abandoning you just after you had him.'

'Oh, Amy.'

She hugged her, told Ben to open the fizzy water and Matt to find glasses, and Amy sat there and cuddled Thomas and wondered how much better it could get.

Two days ago, she'd been in the depths of despair. Now, she was back home, her closest, dearest friends were with her, and she and Matt were going to see if they could make their relationship work.

That still filled her with a certain amount of trepidation, but she knew half of the butterflies were excitement at the prospect, and she tried to forget about it, to put it on one side and concentrate on enjoying the moment.

One day at a time, she told herself yet again, and took a glass of fizzy water from Ben and they toasted the babies. And as she lifted her glass, she met Matt's eyes over the top of it and he winked at her, and she thought, *It's going to be all right. We can do this. We can.*

'That was my parents. They send their love.'

Ben and Daisy had gone home with Thomas and she'd just settled Josh in his crib when Matt came back into the sitting room, slipping his phone into his pocket. She'd heard it ring, and she frowned at what he said. 'They know you're with me?'

'Well, of course they do. Why wouldn't they?'

Why not, indeed? 'Have you told them about the baby?'

He gave a soft, disbelieving laugh. 'Amy, I've just become a father. Of *course* I've told them. I told them days ago.'

Well, of course he had. How stupid of her. They were a very close family, and Ben had just had a baby, too, which they would have been eagerly anticipating, and so they would all have been on the phone frequently. He was lucky to have them. So lucky...

He sat down on the sofa opposite her and searched her eyes. 'Amy, I know you've lost both of your parents, but have you told any members of your family?' he asked gently, and she shook her head.

'Not yet. I didn't want any of them to come over and have hysterics when they saw me, I just didn't need it. It's not as if I ever see my aunt or my cousins. I thought it would be better to tell them when it was all settling down and we knew the baby was all right.'

Not to mention her, he thought, because he'd had a

few hours there where having hysterics wouldn't have been out of the way. 'You have a point. You looked pretty rough at first.'

She laughed, to his surprise. '*I* looked rough? Did you not look in a mirror?'

He smiled acknowledgement. 'Touché,' he said. 'I needed a few hours' sleep and a shave, but you—Amy, you worried me.' His smile faded as he remembered the sheer blind terror that had gripped him when he'd thought she might die.

'Was it really that bad? That close?'

He nodded, and swallowed hard. 'Yes, it was really that close, my love. You scared me half to death. I thought I was going to lose you.'

No wonder she'd been so out of it, she thought. She hadn't realised it had been that bad—although if she'd been thinking clearly she would have worked it out for herself from the state of him and the time that had elapsed and how high her blood pressure had risen.

'Oh, Matt,' she said softly, and he got up and came over to her and sat beside her, tucking his arm round her and dropping a light kiss on her hair.

'It's OK. It's over now, and you're getting better. I'm sorry, I shouldn't have told you. I didn't want to worry you.'

'You didn't—not for me. I know I was in good hands. You and Ben wouldn't have let anything happen to me.'

They might not have had any choice, of course. They both knew that, but by tacit agreement the subject was dropped. Joshua was asleep, Matt had put soft music on and she rested her head against his shoulder and let herself enjoy the moment.

CHAPTER EIGHT

Josh woke at three.

Amy had fed him at eleven, and Matt had changed his nappy, put him in a clean sleepsuit and tucked him up next to her bed in the Moses basket while she'd used the bathroom.

And now he was awake again.

Prising his eyes open, Matt threw off the quilt and went into Amy's room. She was just stirring, about to get out of bed, but she looked sore and uncomfortable, and he tutted and eased her legs back up onto the bed and handed her the baby, tucking a stray lock of hair behind her ear with gentle fingers.

'You feed him, I'll get you a drink. Do you want decaf tea or herbal something, or just cold water?'

She gazed at him a little blankly. 'Tea?' she said hopefully, after a moment. 'Tea would be fabulous if you can be bothered, but you don't have to—'

'Don't argue, Amy. You've had far too much your own way. Now it's my turn to do the worrying.'

He left her alone with the baby, and she stared down at him while he suckled, his eyes firmly fixed on her in the dim light from the landing, his tiny hand splayed across her breast. She slid her thumb under it and it closed around her, and she stroked the back of his hand with her fingers, smiling down at him in wonder.

She was getting used to him now, getting used to how small he was and yet how determined and how very, very good at getting his way.

Just like his father, she thought wryly, and looked up as Matt came into the room and put the tea down on her bedside table.

He hovered for a moment, another cup in his hand, and she sensed he was waiting for the invitation, so she shifted her feet across and patted the edge of the bed. 'Stay,' she said softly, and he smiled, a fleeting quirk of his lips, and sat down at the end of the bed, watching her thoughtfully.

'How's the feeding going?'

'Well. Considering the start he had, he's amazing.'

She tucked her little finger in the corner of his mouth and eased him off, then held him out to Matt.

'Here you are, little one, go to Daddy. Want to wind him? Since you're so good at it,' she added with a smile, so he put his tea down and took the baby, and she shuffled up the bed a bit more and drank her own tea while he walked up and down, rubbing the baby's back. And as he walked, she watched him longingly.

He was dressed—if you could call it that—in soft jersey boxers, and the baby was propped against his bare shoulder, looking impossibly tiny against that broad chest. One large hand was holding him in place, the other stroking his back gently, and the tenderness of the gesture brought tears to her eyes. 'That's my little lager lout,' he said proudly as the baby burped, and she chuckled and blinked the tears away.

Matt turned and caught her eye, still smiling, and then he surprised her.

'Thank you,' he said, serious now, the smile gone, and she frowned at him in confusion.

'For what?'

'For having him? For going through all that alone, when you must have been so frightened. For mistakenly, misguidedly trying to spare me if things had gone wrong again. But not thank you for keeping me out of the loop, because I would have been here for you all along, Amy, if you'd only given me the chance.'

She felt another stab of guilt, but she'd done it for the best reasons and there was no point going over it again. 'Don't be daft, you work in London, you would have just been down there worrying and bullying Ben for hourly updates.'

He smiled wryly and brought the baby back to her side.

'You might be right, but you still should have told me.' The smile faded, and he gave a heavy sigh and ran his hand through his hair, spiking it wildly. He looked tousled and sexy and unbearably dear to her, and she took Josh from him and settled him at the other breast, suddenly self-conscious under his searching gaze.

Not because of the feeding, but because her hair must be all over the place, she had dark bags under her eyes and her tummy still looked like a bag of jelly.

But he didn't look as if he cared. He didn't look as if he was seeing any of that. Instead he gave a fleeting frown, picked up the cups and headed for the door.

'Call me when you're done, I'll change him and put him down for you,' he said, and left her alone.

He took the cups down to the kitchen, put them in

the dishwasher and rested his head against the wall cupboard above it, his hands braced on the edge of the worktop.

He wanted her. Not like that, not at the moment, because she was still recovering from the eclampsia and the surgery. But he was overcome with longing—the longing to get into bed beside her and ease her into his arms and hold her, just hold her while she slept. He'd held her last night, on the sofa, her head on his shoulder and her soft breath teasing his chest in the open neck of his shirt.

It had felt so good to have her in his arms again, so right. But there was still a gulf between them, a wariness on both sides because of all the heartache and grief they'd shared and yet not really shared—and they still hadn't.

They had a long way to go before they could pick up the threads of their old life together, and he knew that, but he was impatient. They had so much going for them, and so much depended on the success of their relationship.

Not least the happiness and well-being of their son.

He heard the boards creak, and with a heavy sigh he pushed away from the worktop and headed upstairs. This he could do. The rest—the rest would come.

They just had to give it time.

Daisy took her stitches out on Saturday morning, which made her a lot more comfortable.

Matt had offered, but somehow it seemed extraordinarily intimate, and Ben was hardly any better, even if he'd put them there after the section and had a professional interest in his handiwork. She still felt uncomfortable about it, so Daisy did it for her, and then they had coffee together in the garden with the babies at their sides. And for the first time in years she felt like a normal woman again, doing the things that normal women did instead of standing on the outside looking in.

There was still a core of pain inside her for the loss of Samuel, and she supposed there always would be, but that was fine. She wouldn't have it any other way. He was still her son, always would be, and she was entitled to her grief.

Thomas started to fuss, so Daisy took him home and Amy left Matt with Josh in his Moses basket and went upstairs and had a look through the things Matt had bought—on her instructions. It seemed she hadn't been thinking quite as clearly as she'd imagined, because it had soon became obvious that the list she'd given him had some vital elements missing.

One of the most important, as Matt had pointed out, was a pram. She was still feeling tender, still walking carefully, but it was a beautiful day, and it would have been a good day for taking him out for a little stroll to the park nearby, only they didn't have a pram.

She. She didn't have a pram. They weren't a 'they' yet and might not ever be, so she'd be crazy to let herself start thinking like that.

There were also other things—very personal things— that she needed, and there was no way she was asking him, obstetrician or not! And it wasn't fair to keep asking Daisy...

He appeared in the doorway, tapping lightly and sticking his head round. 'Somebody needs his mum,' he began, and then took one look at her and said, 'What's the matter?'

'What makes you think something's the matter?' she asked, taking the baby from him, and he laughed.

'The look on your face? You're like an open book, Amy. So come on, let's have it.'

'I need to go shopping.'

His eyebrows shot up. 'Shopping?'

'For baby stuff. I was thinking, it would be nice to go out for a walk with the baby, but we don't have a pram.'

He rolled his eyes and sat down on the bed, sprawling back against the pillows as if he belonged there. Sadly not...

'You're going to take me pram shopping, aren't you?' he said faintly, and she started to laugh.

'You great big wuss, you can cope with it!'

'Twice? Dear God. I tell you, I shall have a lot more respect for women in future!' He tipped his head on one side and his face gentled. 'Are you sure you're up to it?' he asked softly. 'It's only been eight days.'

'I think so. I'll be careful.'

'Too right you'll be careful. I'll make sure of it. So when do you want to go?'

She sighed. 'I'd say as soon as I've fed him, but that seems to be pretty unreliable as an indicator of how long we've got before he wants more.'

'He's hungry. He's catching up.'

'Well, at least he eats like you and doesn't pick at his food!' she teased. 'Head down, get on with it, get it over.'

He smiled. 'It's only because I've spent so many years in hospitals and if you want hot food you have to grab the chance. So, if you feed him now and I make us something to eat while you do that, and then we make a dash for it as soon as he's done, we've probably got long enough to get part-way through the first pram demonstration—'

She threw a pillow at him, which was silly because it hurt her incision, but it was satisfying.

He caught it, put it down and shook his head.

'Steady, now. No pillow fights.'

Her breath hitched. They'd had a pillow fight once, and she'd lost—if you could call it that. She'd ended up under him, pinned to the bed by his long, solid leg across her, her hands manacled above her head by his firm, strong fingers, and he'd slowly and thoroughly plundered her body.

Matt watched her from the bed, his heart thudding slowly, the memory that was written clearly across her face still fresh in his mind. He'd held her down, and slowly and thoroughly explored every inch of her, and she'd loved every second of it—

Josh began to cry in earnest, yanking him back to reality, and he got off the bed and headed for the door. 'Why don't you feed him and I'll make you a drink and something to eat, and then we can go.'

He left her to it, getting out before he said or did something inappropriate, and as he reached the bottom of the stairs he heard her door close softly. He let his breath out, went into the kitchen and put the kettle on, and stared blankly into the fridge.

They needed a supermarket shop—and he needed an urgent appointment with a psychiatrist. Thinking about Amy lying naked beneath him was hardly the most sensible or intelligent thing for him to focus on at the moment—or ever, possibly.

He made some sandwiches—cheese and pickle, be-

cause that was about all there was and she could do with
the calcium—and then carried them up to her.

He'd seen her breastfeeding loads of times, but suddenly—because of the pillow fight remark?—it took on
a whole new dimension. He put the plate and cup down
on the bedside table next to her and left her to it, taking
his out into the conservatory so he could try to focus
on something other than Amy and her body.

The pram shopping was every bit as mind-boggling and
confusing as it had been the first time, but Amy took it
in her stride. It seemed to make sense to her—women,
he thought, must be hard-wired to that kind of stuff—
and within an hour she'd chosen a travel system that
seemed to do everything except fold itself.

And it had a baby seat that used the same base he had
for his car, which meant greater flexibility. Excellent.
It would be delivered on Monday morning, and all they
needed now were the other things on her list, so she sent
him off with Josh to browse.

'I need some things for me,' she said, colouring
slightly in an endearing way that made him want to
smile. He restrained himself until he'd turned away, just
nodded and left her to it, the baby seat hanging from his
hand. He was getting used to it, to the looks they were
getting, the oohs and aahs because Josh was so tiny—
and such a beautiful baby. Or was that just paternal
pride? He looked down and met those staggering blue
eyes staring up at him, and beamed. Nah. He was gorgeous. The pride was justified.

He glanced back and saw her examining a nursing
bra, and he closed his eyes and tried not to think about
her body. Inappropriate. Concentrate.

He took Josh to look at cots instead—travel cots, for starters, so they could take him down to London with them and stay in his house there on occasions. He hadn't discussed it with Amy, but he knew it was a possibility, so he found the same assistant who'd been so helpful over the buggy and was talked through the folding cots.

And it dawned on him very rapidly that this baby, tiny though he might be, was going to make a significant difference to his life. Starting with his car.

He sighed. He'd only had it four months, but it simply wouldn't fit all the paraphernalia of a baby on the move.

He glanced across at the underwear department and spotted her at the till. Good, because they had a lot to do. Or he did. Starting with the joys of the supermarket, and leading on to a little light surfing of estate cars on the internet.

His phone beeped at him, and he slid it out of his pocket and frowned at the screen. It was a text from Ben, telling him that their parents were coming down tomorrow for a flying visit. He blew out his breath, estate cars forgotten. He'd thought they were leaving it till next weekend, but apparently not. He glanced across at Amy again. He wasn't sure if she was up to such an emotional and stressful day. Not yet, but if they were coming down especially…

And then just to complicate it even further, Josh started to cry. He swung the baby seat by the handle, long slow swings to rock him off again, but he wasn't having any and Matt gave in.

'Come along, little man, let's go and find your mummy,' he said, and headed towards the tills.

She heard them coming, the new-baby cry going

straight to her breasts and making them prickle. Damn.
She'd forgotten breast pads. 'Over there,' the assistant
said, and she grabbed a box and put it on the pile.

'I've just had a text from my parents,' he said as he
arrived from her side, and she felt a sudden flurry of
nerves. She hadn't seen them since Ben and Daisy's
wedding, she hadn't spoken to them yet, and she wasn't
at all sure she could cope with it.

'Where are they staying? You're in my spare room
and Ben and Daisy have got Florence for the weekend.'

'I don't know that they are. I think it's a flying visit,
because they have to have someone to look after the
dogs. I think they were talking about coming down to
see Thomas next weekend, but they've obviously just
brought it forwards.'

'I didn't even know it was on the cards,' she pointed
out, and he smiled wryly.

'Nor did I, really. Mum just sprang it on me. It'll be
OK, though, I'll get some biscuits or something while
I'm at the supermarket and you can just sit there and
drink tea and let them admire him. They're thrilled,
Amy, really thrilled, and you won't have to do anything.'

Was that what he thought? That she was worried
about having to do things? She wasn't, not at all, but
apart from a brief hug and a fleeting exchange at the
wedding, the last conversation she'd had with his mother
had been after she'd lost Samuel, and for all his reassurance that they were thrilled, she wondered if it would
be a little awkward because she'd kept Josh a secret.

Oh, this was so hard! She thanked the assistant,
scooped up her shopping and headed for the door, Matt
at her side with the now-screaming baby. She fed him
in the back of the car, sitting in the car park, and then

they drove straight home and he dropped her off with Josh and went shopping, leaving her alone.

It was the first time he'd left her since she'd come out of hospital, she realised, except for odd trips to the corner shop, and she was glad to have a little peace and quiet.

Not that he was noisy, exactly, but having him there was just—disturbing? As if there was an electric current running through her all the time, making her tingle.

She changed Josh's nappy, and the baby, full and contented, didn't even stir as she put him in the Moses basket. And the bed looked so inviting. Could she snatch half an hour?

Sure she could. Why not?

She slipped off her shoes, climbed onto the bed fully clothed and fell straight asleep.

The house was in silence when he got back. He'd put the car in the car port at the back, and carried the shopping through to the kitchen via the conservatory, so he hadn't used the front door, which was right under her bedroom.

Maybe she hadn't heard him come in—and maybe she was resting?

He crept upstairs as quietly as he could and stuck his head round the door, to find her lying curled on the bed, fast asleep, the baby flat out in the Moses basket next to her. It made him smile, but it brought a lump to his throat as well.

How was it possible to love someone so small so very, very much? And so soon? Or still to love a woman for all these years, even though she'd made it clear she didn't want to spend her life with him? Or hadn't. Maybe now it would be different, but maybe only because of Josh.

Maybe if she changed her mind now, it would be for practical reasons, perhaps the same reasons she'd agreed to marry him last time? And as soon as that reason had no longer existed, she'd called off the wedding.

She surely wouldn't have done that if she'd loved him.

He backed out of the room and went downstairs, his heart suddenly heavy. He'd managed to convince himself that it was going to be wonderful, but now he felt a flicker of doubt.

Well, more than a flicker. Oh, hell.

He needed to *do* something, something concrete rather than wandering around on a knife edge. If the garden hadn't been largely paved, he'd go and dig it or mow the lawn or something, but there was nothing to do.

But there was something he could do, something he needed to do, no matter what happened with him and Amy, because he had a son, regardless, and that was already making its impact felt.

He'd put the kettle on already, so he made himself tea, went out into the conservatory with his laptop and started researching estate cars.

They heard his parents arrive the next day—the sound of the doorbell ringing faintly in the distance, the cries of delight as they went through to the garden and found Daisy there with the baby.

She met Matt's eyes, and he smiled reassuringly and gave her hand a quick squeeze.

'It'll be fine,' he promised her.

It was. He gave them twenty minutes, then got to his feet and headed for the garden, dropping a fleeting kiss on her head in passing. She could see him as he stuck his head over the fence and grinned. 'Permission to come aboard?' he asked, and Ben opened the gate in the fence to let him through.

She could hear them laughing, hear the warmth of their greeting from her seat in the conservatory, and her palms felt suddenly prickly with nerves. She hoped—she desperately hoped—that they wouldn't come as a tribe, all the Walker clan in force to overwhelm her.

She should have known Liz, of all people, would have had more common sense. Matt's mother slipped quietly through the gate on her own, came into the conservatory and bent to gather Amy into her arms for a motherly hug.

'Oh, it's so good to see you,' she said softly, then let her go and sat beside her, holding her hand. 'How are you? Matthew said you'd had a dreadful time.'

She gave a quiet laugh. 'Apparently. I don't really remember very much about it.'

Liz smiled. 'Lucky you, from what I gather. You had both my boys worried there. And are you OK now?'

She nodded. 'I think so. Getting there.'

'And the baby?'

'Pick him up, see for yourself. He's about to wake up anyway.'

'Sure?'

She smiled, feeling herself relax. Liz was a midwife, too, and she knew she could trust her absolutely with her precious son. 'Sure,' she echoed, and Liz turned back the little cover and pressed her fingers to her lips, her eyes flooding.

'Oh, he's so tiny! Oh, bless his little heart, what a beautiful baby. Oh, Amy. You must be overjoyed.'

She nodded, but then for some inexplicable reason

she started to cry, and Liz crouched beside her, rubbing her back and making soothing noises.

'Oh, sweetheart,' she murmured. 'It must have been so scary for you on your own—you're a silly girl, you should have told us, we could have looked after you. I could have come down.'

She sniffed and stared at her, the tears welling again at her kindness. 'Why would you do that?'

'Oh, poppet, do you need to ask? You were going to be my daughter, and I've never forgotten you. I've worried about you all these years, and I worried about you at the wedding, too. I could see how strong the pull was between you—and to be honest I never believed that cock-and-bull story of Matthew's about getting something from his room. A blind man could have seen the way it was with you that night, and it was only going to end one way. It was what might happen afterwards that worried me most, because I thought it had the capacity to hurt you both dreadfully, and I wasn't sure who I was most worried about, you or him.'

'Why would you worry about me? He's your son.'

'Because you left so much unfinished business between you,' she said quietly. 'So much sorrow and pain. And I don't know about you, but I don't think Matthew's ever really dealt with it.'

She nodded. 'I think you're right. I don't think either of us have really dealt with it.'

'You need to. And Joshua will help you—he'll help to heal you.'

'He already is,' she said, her eyes going automatically to her little son. His legs were starting to go, his arms flailing, and any moment now he'd begin to wail. 'I think he needs a cuddle with his grannie,' she said softly, and Liz got to her feet again and picked him up, crooning to him as she cradled him in her arms and introduced herself to him.

'Oh, he's so like Matthew.'

'Not Ben?'

She laughed. 'Not so much, no. They were different, even at Josh's age—but only I could see it. He lies in the same way, with his arms flung up. Ben never did that.'

He started to grizzle and turn his head towards her, and Liz smiled and held him out to her. 'Yours, I think,' she said, and handed him over. 'That's the wonderful thing about being a grandmother, so I'm told. You just hand them back when they need attention.'

Why on earth had she worried?

They were lovely. The visit was only short, and they all ended up having lunch under the tree in Ben and Daisy's garden, the two proud grandparents cuddling the babies in turn while Amy sat with Daisy and enjoyed the luxury of being redundant for a few hours.

Florence was there, too, pushing her own 'baby' round in its buggy, and she announced that Mummy was having a new baby for her, so she'd have two brothers soon. She seemed utterly delighted at the idea, and she was sweet with the babies, and with Daisy.

And there it was again, the knowledge that Samuel was missing from the scene. He would have been a little older than Florence, and Amy could imagine them playing, the four children growing up together. But it would never be...

'What's up?'

Matt's voice was soft in her ear, and she turned her head and found him crouched behind her, her eyes searching. 'Nothing,' she lied, but his smile told her he knew she was lying.

'Can I get you anything?'

She shook her head. 'Actually, I think I might have a lie down. I'm feeling tired.'

He laughed softly. 'Me, too. These ruptured nights are a bit wearing.'

'Ruptured?' she said with a smile, and he smiled back and leant over and kissed her cheek.

'You know what I mean,' he said, and straightened up. 'I'll take him, Dad. I think he probably needs feeding, and Amy's ready for a rest, so we'll leave you to it. Thanks for coming, it's been lovely to see you.'

'Come up soon,' his mother said, and he nodded, but he wasn't making any promises. It all depended on Amy, and Harrogate—well, Harrogate held all manner of memories.

They were hugged and kissed, and then they made their escape. And somehow, after she'd fed him and Matt had put him back in the Moses basket in the bedroom, he ended up lying down on the bed next to her, the soft sound of his breathing somehow soothing.

'I'm glad they came,' she murmured. 'It was so nice to see them again. Your mother was lovely to me.'

He turned his head. 'Why wouldn't she be?'

'No reason. She's been worried about me, apparently.'

'Of course she has. We all have.'

'She's worried about you, too.'

He sighed. 'She's got a point, Amy. We're both in limbo, have been for years.'

He turned so he was facing her, lying on his side just inches away, his head propped on his hand. 'Why don't you come back with me to London tomorrow for a couple of days? I only have to pop into the hospital for a short while, and you could sit in my garden and watch the birds while I'm out, and then we can take Josh for a walk in the park.'

She frowned. 'You don't have a garden.'

'Yes, I do—I don't live in the flat any more. I thought you realised that. I moved to a mews cottage just a few doors from Rob.'

That surprised her. They'd often visited his friend, and she'd always said how much she loved his house. It wasn't large, but it had a garage and a garden, unusually for London, and the little cobbled lane that ran between two streets was filled with flowers and potted plants outside the houses.

They'd even talked about moving there, but then she'd lost the baby and everything had stopped.

Except he'd done it, anyway, bought one of the houses and was living their dream alone.

Why?

Because it had made economic sense, or because he hadn't been able to let the dream go?

Only one way to find out.

'That sounds lovely,' she said, feeling—excited? Maybe. She hadn't felt excited about anything in this way for years, and she smiled at him. 'Really lovely. How did you know I had cabin fever?'

He smiled back and reached out a hand, touching her face. It was the lightest touch, the merest whisper of his fingers over her cheek, but it set all her senses on fire, and for a breathless, endless moment she was frozen there, eyes locked with his, her entire body motionless.

And then he dropped his hand and rolled off the bed.

'I'll leave you to rest. I've got things to do. Give me a call if you need anything.'

Only you, she thought, but she said nothing.

It was too soon, and this time, she was going to make absolutely sure of what she was doing before she committed herself to Matt again.

CHAPTER NINE

THEY left for London after the travel system was delivered.

Matt spent an hour trying to work out how to put it all together, then eventually, temper fraying, managed to get the frame and the carrycot into the boot of his car. There was no room for their luggage except on the back seat beside the baby, and he frowned at it.

There was nowhere else he could put it, so he made sure there was nothing heavy loose in the cabin, squashed their bags behind the seats and resolved to get an estate car at the first possible opportunity.

Tomorrow would be good.

Then as soon as he was fed and changed, they strapped Josh into the car seat and set off.

'It's like going on an expedition to the Antarctic,' he grumbled, sounding so exasperated and confused that Amy laughed.

He shot her a dirty look, sighed and then joined in, his bad mood evaporating rapidly. Why would he be grumpy? The woman he loved was in the seat beside him, his baby son was in the back, and they were going to see the house where he hoped—please God not in vain—that they'd live together.

No. He wasn't grumpy. He was just driving the wrong car. Easily fixable. The accommodation issue was far harder, and he ran his eye mentally over the house. Was it clean? Tidy? He'd issued the invitation without a thought, but he couldn't remember how he'd left it and his cleaner came in once a fortnight. Had she been?

No idea. The days since Josh had burst into his life had blurred together so he didn't have a clue where he was any more. With Josh and Amy, he told himself. That was the only thing that mattered. The state of the house was irrelevant.

The house was lovely.

It was just a few doors from Rob's, and it was bigger, the one they'd often talked about because it looked tatty and run-down and in need of love.

Well, not any more. It looked immaculate, the sash windows all renovated, by the look of it, the brass on the front door gleaming, and she couldn't wait to see what he'd done to it, especially the garden. It had had the most amazing wisteria, she remembered, sprawling all over the garden. Had he been able to save it? He pressed a button on his key fob and the roller-shutter on his garage door slid quietly up out of the way, and he drove in and cut the engine.

'Home,' he said with satisfaction, and she felt a strange and disorientating sense of loss. How odd. She had a home. Except of course it wasn't hers, not really. She was only living there on a temporary basis, on Ben's insistence, but now that Matt was back in her life, there was no need for that.

'What's up?'

She opened her mouth to tell him, and thought better

of it. 'Nothing,' she said. 'It's the house we used to talk about. You didn't tell me that. It took me by surprise.'

'It didn't look like a very nice surprise,' he said quietly, and she realised he sounded—what? Disappointed?

'It's a lovely surprise,' she assured him. 'I can't wait to see it.'

'I can't guarantee what it's like, it might be a tip,' he warned, unclipping Josh's seat and heading for a door. 'Come on in.'

It was beautiful. They went straight into the kitchen, a light and airy room with doors out into the garden. There was a sofa at one end, and a television, and she guessed he used this room more than any other. She could see why, with the garden just there, and it looked lovely. Far less overgrown, of course, but lush and inviting, a real oasis in the middle of the city. It was a little smaller than Daisy's, and the painted brick walls that surrounded it gave it a delightfully secret feel.

He opened the doors and they went out, and she could hear birds singing and smell the most heavenly scent—from the old wisteria scrambling up the back wall of the house.

'You saved it!'

His mouth twisted into a smile, and he reached out a hand and touched her cheek. 'I had to keep it after everything you'd said about it. It reminded me of you.'

What could she say to that? Nothing. She was picking her way through a minefield again, and she felt suddenly slightly nervous. 'Can I see the rest?'

'Sure.'

He left the doors open, and they went past a cloakroom and upstairs to the hall. The front door came in there, accessed from the mews by old stone steps that she'd noticed were covered in pots, and off the front of the hall was a study, and behind it a sitting room.

'You haven't got a dining room,' she said, and he gave a wry smile.

'I don't really need one. I've got a breakfast bar, and I eat there. I don't really entertain like that. Come and see the bedrooms.'

She followed him up and found three rooms, two small ones over the front, and a larger one, obviously his, next to the bathroom at the back.

'It's lovely, Matt. Really, really nice. I love the colours.'

'Yes, they're your sort of colours,' he said softly, and she noticed he wasn't smiling. Why? And why put it like that, as if he'd chosen the colours because she'd like them—unless…?

'I'm glad you like it. I was sort of hoping that maybe one day you might—' He broke off, shrugged and turned away, heading back down the stairs. 'Tea?'

'Sounds lovely.' *Might what?* She followed him thoughtfully.

'Why don't you have a potter round the kitchen and make us some tea while I bring in all the luggage?' he suggested, putting Josh down on the floor by the sofa, and she filled the kettle and searched through the cupboards.

It was logically organised, as she might have expected from Matt. Mugs over the kettle, tea and coffee beside them in the next cupboard, cutlery in the drawer underneath.

Nice mugs, she thought. Plain white bone china. She looked around, frowning slightly. The kitchen was the sort of kitchen she'd fantasised about, a hand-built painted Shaker kitchen, with granite worktops and integrated appliances. The garden was heavy with the scent of the wisteria she'd said she loved. Everything about it—*everything*—was how she would have done it.

Had he done it for her? she wondered, and she felt her eyes fill with tears.

'You haven't got very far with the tea.'

She switched the kettle on to boil again and reached for the mugs. 'When did you buy the house?' she asked, turning to look at him, and he went still.

'Um—it came on the market just after…'

'After we lost Samuel,' she finished for him softly.

He nodded. 'I thought…' He shook his head. 'It doesn't matter.'

'I think it does. I think it matters a lot.'

He let his breath out very slowly, and turned to face her, his eyes wary and yet revealing. 'I hoped—one day—that you might come back to me. That we might live here, together, as we'd talked about. Build a new life, start again. Then I realised it wasn't going to happen, but I finished it anyway, because it was handy for the hospital and—well, I loved it.'

She didn't know what to say, because it hadn't been an invitation, as such, more a statement of why and how he'd done it. And she wasn't sure if it was still current, if the hope was still alive. And if it was, she wasn't sure what her answer would be, so she just nodded slowly, and turned her back on him and made the tea, and by the time she'd finished, he'd found some biscuits and taken Josh out into the garden so they could sit near the wisteria and soak up the last of the sunshine.

The subject was dropped, and he talked instead about work, about the people she'd known and what they were doing, that Rob was married now and had a child, a little girl of one, and another on the way, and how Tina, one of the other midwives, had finally convinced her registrar boyfriend to marry her—lightweight gossip that distracted her from the delicate subject of their relationship.

Then Josh woke, starving hungry and indignant, and she fed him, the sudden blissful silence broken only by the twittering of the birds and the muted hum of the traffic in the distance.

'I need to do some work,' Matt said suddenly, getting up. 'Make yourself at home. I'll be down in a while.'

She nodded, but he'd already gone, heading upstairs to his study, no doubt, and leaving her alone to ponder on his motivation and what, if anything, this new information might mean to her.

He stood upstairs at the sitting room window, staring down at her and wondering why he'd brought her here.

He'd been longing to, for years now, but at least before he couldn't actually picture her here. Now, though, her image would be everywhere, her presence almost tangible in every room. If this didn't work out...

It had to work out. There was no acceptable alternative—at least not to him. Not one he could live with.

He dialled the hospital number and asked them to page his registrar and get him to call him, then he stood there staring broodingly down at her until the phone rang. Only then did he take his eyes off her, go into the study, shut the door and concentrate on work. At least that was something he had some control over.

* * *

They stayed in London for two days, and for Amy they were idyllic.

She spent a lot of time in the garden with Josh, and when Matt was there they walked to the little park just two streets away. It had a playground for little children, and she found herself imagining bringing Josh here when he was older.

Which was silly, because she lived in Suffolk, not London. It was where her job was, and just because Matt had hoped she'd come back to him five years ago didn't mean they were going to make it work now.

Which meant Matt would be bringing Josh here on his own at the weekends, she realised, and felt suddenly incredibly sad.

He'd been taking photos of her with the baby in the park, sitting under the trees and strolling with the buggy, and she took the camera from him and photographed them together, the two men in her life—except Matt might not be.

There was still a wariness about him, a distance from her, and she wasn't sure why it was. Protecting himself from further hurt? She could understand that, but the image of him playing here alone with his son was too awful to contemplate.

Going back to Yoxburgh was strange, and not necessarily in a good way.

They quickly settled, though, and Matt went back to London in the middle of Saturday night because they'd had a multiple pregnancy admitted and the staff were worried about the babies.

He came back on Tuesday, having delivered the triplets, and he was sombre.

'We lost one,' he told her, when she asked, and she wished she hadn't—which was ridiculous, because she worked as a midwife, she knew these things happened.

But he looked gutted, and for the first time really she wondered how *he* dealt with stillbirth, not from the patients' viewpoint but his own.

'I'm sorry,' she said, hugging him, and he held her close for a moment, his head rested against hers, drawing strength from her. God, he needed her. He'd missed her, the last few days interminable without her and Josh, and sad though he was, it was good to be home.

Home? he thought. This wasn't home! This was Amy's home, and he had to remember that. He was getting too comfortable. Too settled.

And in too deep.

They went backwards and forwards between London and Yoxburgh for the next three weeks, the journey being made much easier by the fact that he'd changed his car for an estate version, so at least she knew he was serious about being a hands-on father. Very hands on. He got up in the night almost without fail and made her tea, staying to chat while she fed Josh and then change him and settle him again, and when she was exhausted he sent her back to bed in the day and did everything except the breast feeds. And gradually she grew stronger and fitter, her incision felt almost normal and she started talking about going back to work.

Matt was astounded. 'You can't! How can you do that? You've been ill—you've had a section!'

'Matt, I'm fine! I'm all right now, and I have no choice. If I don't work, I've got no way of paying my living expenses.'

'I'll pay you maintenance.'

'Why should you?'

'Because he's my son?'

She shook her head. 'That's different, but I need to earn a living for me. I don't need maintenance from you for that, I can cope on my salary—'

'Only because Ben and Daisy aren't charging you the proper rent for this house.'

She stared at him, stunned. 'Matt, they won't take it! I've offered, but they won't take any more.'

'Only because they know you haven't got it, and that's unfair, Amy, it's taking advantage of their friendship and good nature, and it's costing them hundreds of pounds every month.'

She felt her mouth hanging open, and shut it. Of course it was—she knew that, but she'd avoided thinking about it. Now he'd brought it so forcibly to her attention, she was gutted. They'd seemed to want her there so much—and because she'd needed the house, she hadn't challenged it hard enough, she'd taken their argument about being choosy about their tenant at face value.

'They said they wanted me,' she said, shocked, and he shrugged.

'They do, and they can have you. They can have you, Amy, but at the proper rent, and I'll pay you maintenance so you can afford to live here. But what about Josh? You haven't answered that one yet. What'll happen to him when you go back to work?'

'I'll put him in the crèche.'

'Have you booked? Because places are usually tight, and it's tricky with shift work. And childcare is hideously expensive. Are you sure you can afford it? Have you looked into the costs?'

No, of course she hadn't. She hadn't done any of it because she hadn't dared to believe it would be all right, and now she felt sick with worry and shame and guilt towards Ben and Daisy. She bit her lip, and he shook his head and sighed.

'Amy, do you *really* want to go back to work so soon? Or is this a purely economic decision? Because if it is, you don't have to work if you don't want to. I can afford to support you, but I want to be part of his life, and part of yours. And if you moved back to London, we could do all of that. It would be amazing. You've said you like my house, and we could live there and you could be at home with him and enjoy his babyhood, and I'd get to see him growing up.'

It was the obvious answer, of course. If she lived with him, it would cost him hardly anything to support her, and he'd be with his son. But how much of it was to do with her and how much he loved her?

Because he'd never said those words, in all these weeks of talking and getting to know each other again. Never once had he said he loved her, or tried in any way to touch her, kiss her, hold her in anything other than a supportive way.

And she realised she had no idea at all where she stood.

'What happens when something goes wrong, Matt? If I leave behind my job, my home, my friends—I'd have to start again. I've done that once. Believe me, I don't want to do it again.'

'What makes you think anything would go wrong?'

'Experience,' she said quietly, and to her relief Josh woke at that moment and she had a legitimate excuse to leave the room.

* * *

He didn't say any more about it that day, and the following day he left her in Suffolk and went back to London
on his own. Maybe, he thought, it was time to let her
cope alone for a while, ease himself out of her life and
let her see what it was like.

He was helping her with all nappy changing and bath-
ing, he did all the shopping, all the housework, he wa-
tered the garden and weeded the flowerbeds and washed
her car and cleaned the windows—mostly to fill the
time between feeds because he didn't trust himself not
to rush her if he was alone with her. She'd been so ill,
was still getting over major surgery, whatever she might
say to the contrary, and the last thing she needed was
him coming on to her.

So he took himself off out of her life, and rattled
round his house alone and missed her every single minute he wasn't at work.

And then he got to work one morning and checked
the calendar.

It was the date they'd lost Samuel, he realised with
shock. He'd never forgotten it before, never overlooked
it. He was always in Harrogate on that day, always took
flowers to the cemetery, but this time he had Amy to
think about, and maybe it was time they confronted this
issue together, today of all days.

He cleared his workload, delegated his clinics and
left London, arriving back at Amy's house in Yoxburgh
without warning and finding her sitting in the conservatory in tears. He'd let himself in with his keys, and
he wondered if he should have done or if she minded.

'Hey,' he said softly, crouching down and touching
her face with a gentle hand. 'It's OK, I'm here now.'

'I'm all right,' she lied, and he knew she wasn't, because her face was blotched and tearstained and her eyes were swollen and she was in a sea of soggy tissues.

He knew just how she felt. He'd done the same thing every year, but this year he'd been more worried about her, and he scooped her up and carried her into the sitting room and cradled her on his lap as she cried.

Then finally she sniffed to halt and tried to sit up, but he wouldn't let her, just held her against his chest and she gave in and rested her head on his shoulder and laid her hand over his heart.

Could she feel that it was broken?

She looked up at him, and with a soft sigh she wiped away his tears. 'When is it going to end?'

He kissed her gently, his lips tasting the salt of her tears, and he sighed quietly.

'I don't know. I don't know if it'll ever truly go.'

She closed her eyes, and the welling tears slid down her cheeks, breaking his heart still further. 'I just wish I had somewhere to go—a focus for my grief. Somewhere I could go and remember him, once in a while. All I've got is the scan photo and my armband from the hospital. Nothing else.'

'There is something else,' he said softly, kicking himself for never thinking of it, never telling her, never sharing their grief. If only he'd known how she felt, if only he'd thought about it. 'I asked the hospital to arrange his cremation, and I went to the...' He couldn't say funeral. 'To the service,' he went on, after a moment. 'The hospital chaplain said a few words, and they scattered his ashes in the garden there. I go every year and put flowers in the garden, but they wrote his name in the Book of Remembrance, and I'm sure you can view it. I'm so sorry, I should have told you, but I'd just put it out of my mind.'

She stared at him blankly. 'There's a book with his name in it? Can we see it?'

He nodded. 'I think so. I'm pretty sure you can. I'll have to phone, but I think so.'

'Phone them now. Please, Matt, phone them now! It's only eleven o'clock. Maybe we could go today.'

He used his phone to find the number, and rang. Half an hour later they were heading north on their way to Yorkshire, the baby fed, Amy's clothes packed haphazardly, but that wasn't what mattered. What mattered was that they were together, today, and anything else was irrelevant.

The book was open at the date, and she ran her finger down the page and found the entry.

Samuel Radcliffe Walker, beloved son of Amy and Matthew. Always in our hearts.

The words swam in front of her eyes, and she sagged against Matt, his arm firmly around her, supporting her. Joshua was on his chest in a baby sling, fast asleep against his father's heart, next to the cherished memory of their other son, and she laid her hand against the baby's back, making the connection.

'I thought he'd been forgotten,' she whispered.

His arm tightened slightly, and she felt his lips brush her hair. 'No. No, Amy, he'll never be forgotten. He'll always be our first son.'

She nodded, her finger tracing the words once more, and then she nodded again and turned away.

'Thank you—thank you so much,' she said to the kindly man who'd shown them the book. He was hovering quietly behind them, giving them space, and Matt shook his hand and thanked him, and led her back outside into the sunshine.

'Where are his ashes?' she asked unsteadily, and Matt showed her the place. He'd never seen the book, but every year he'd brought beautiful cottage garden flowers from a lady who sold them from a little barrow outside her cottage just down the road—real flowers, not a stiff arrangement of scentless hothouse blooms.

They'd bought some on the way here today, and Amy kissed them, then laid them on the grass, taking a moment to remember him and say goodbye, then she straightened up and snuggled against Matt's side, his arm automatically going around her holding her close. He pressed his lips to her hair, and she rested her head against his shoulder as they stood for a moment staring at them, and then she sighed and turned away and they strolled quietly along the paths in the sunshine, arms around each other, hanging on.

They found a bench and sat down, by tacit agreement, not quite ready to leave just yet.

'Are you all right?' he asked softly.

'Mmm. You?'

He smiled wryly. 'I'll do.'

'Thank you—for bringing me here, for coming to see me. I'm not normally that bad. It seemed worse this year, somehow.'

'Mmm. Maybe it's having Josh. It sort of underlines what we've lost,' he said, his voice unsteady, and she nodded.

'I'm so glad we came. I feel so much better now—as if I've done something I've been waiting all these years to do. And I'm glad you were there for his funeral. How did you do that?' she asked, bewildered. 'I wouldn't have been strong enough. How did you cope?'

He gave a hollow little laugh. 'I didn't really. Mum offered to come, but I wanted to do it alone. I didn't want anyone seeing me like that. I was in denial, and if nobody saw me, I could pretend it wasn't happening.'

'That was why I ran away to India,' she admitted. 'So nobody I knew would see me as I fell apart.'

'You were in India?'

'Yes. I went backpacking on my own. Probably not the most sensible thing, but while I was there I spent a couple of weeks living on the fringe of a village where the child mortality rate was dreadful, so it put it in perspective.'

'I'll bet. Amy, I had no idea. I thought you were somewhere in London, one of the other hospitals. I didn't try to find out, either. I thought, if you didn't want me, there was no point in pursuing it.'

She turned and looked at him, seeing the pain in his eyes, and she shook her head slowly. 'It wasn't that I didn't want you, it was that I felt you didn't want me.'

He gave a soft grunt of laughter. 'Oh, I wanted you, Amy. I've never stopped wanting you. I just didn't know how to talk to you, how to deal with it. Mum suggested bereavement counselling, but I turned it down flat because I didn't want to be made to think about it.' He touched her face, his fingers gentle, and his eyes were filled with sorrow.

'I let you down. I'm sorry.'

'I let you down, too. I should have stayed in England, talked to you instead of letting you shut yourself away. I never wanted to end our relationship, Matt, I just couldn't cope with the idea of a party. That great big wedding, with all our family and friends all gathered there just weeks after we'd lost him—it seemed wrong, somehow. It would have been wrong.'

He nodded. 'It would, but I wasn't sure then if it would ever be right, or if we'd lost each other as well along the way. And then you disappeared off the face of the earth, and I bought the house, in case you changed your mind and decided you wanted me after all, but you never did. You'd handed in your notice, and you were gone.'

'You could have found me. I'm a registered midwife, you could have tracked me down.'

He smiled. 'Probably not legally, but I wasn't sure I wanted to. You knew where I was. I thought, when you were ready, you'd come back to me, but you never did, and I gave up hope.'

'And then Ben met Daisy, and there you were again in my life,' she said softly. 'And now we have another son.'

'We do, and I have a feeling he has rising damp,' he said with a smile.

She laughed quietly and felt the edge of his little shorts. 'Oops. I think you might be right.'

'Can you cope with my parents?' he asked, his eyes concerned, and she smiled and nodded.

'Yes. Yes, I can cope with them. I'd love to see them. Can they cope with us, though?'

'I'm sure they can.'

They were overjoyed to see them.

There were more tears, and tea, and lots of hugs, and then they offered to babysit so Matt could take Amy out for dinner.

'Go and have a quiet meal somewhere by yourselves. We can cope. You can express some milk and we can feed him if he wakes.'

'We haven't got any bottles,' Amy said, but Liz had an answer.

'Ben and Daisy have been up here and they brought a steriliser and some bottles with them so we could look after Thomas. Now what else are you going to come up with as an excuse?' she teased, and Amy laughed.

'Nothing. Thank you. Dinner out with Matt would be lovely.'

'In which case, if you'll excuse me, I have a phone call to make,' Matt said, and he dropped a kiss in Amy's palm, closed her fingers over it to keep it safe and with a little wink he walked out with a spring in his stride she hadn't seen for years.

'Right. Let's get these bottles sterilised,' Liz said. 'I don't want you two having any excuses for coming home early.'

CHAPTER TEN

'WHICH rooms do you want us to have?'

His mother searched his eyes, and he lifted his shoulders in an almost invisible shrug, but she understood, it seemed, because she just smiled.

'Yours and Ben's are already made up, and the crib's in Ben's already.'

He nodded. They had a communicating door, which would mean he could help Amy with Josh in the night— and if things went the way he hoped, they'd only need his room.

He took the luggage up, opened the windows and stood staring out over the familiar countryside and breathing in the glorious fresh air. He loved London, loved his job, but it was good to come home.

'Matt?'

He turned and smiled at Amy. 'Hi. I've put your things in Ben's room with Josh's. There's a changing mat in there, and the crib, which might make life easier.'

She looked at the crib, rocking it gently with one finger, memories washing over her. It was one of two that Matt's father had made for their boys, and Liz had shown them to her when she'd been pregnant with Samuel. 'The baby will be able to sleep in one when you come and stay,' she'd said, only Samuel had never needed a crib, and now his brother and his cousin would be sleeping in them.

She waited for the wave of pain, but there was only a gentle sorrow, a quiet acceptance that this was the way things were, and now she could move on, with Josh— and Matt?

She felt a tingle of anticipation, and turned to find him standing in the doorway, watching her.

'OK?'

She nodded. 'Yes. So—where are we going for dinner?'

He smiled. 'A place Ben recommended. It's—um— it's quite smart,' he said, 'but you're about the same size as Mum. I wonder if she's got anything you could borrow?'

She looked down at her baggy jersey dress and leggings, soft and comfortable and easy to wear, but not exactly smart dining. 'Let's hope so or you might be cancelling the reservation!' she said lightly, and went to find Liz.

'Oh, gosh—right. Um—come and see. I'm sure I've got something.'

She had. A lovely black lace dress, soft and stretchy and elegant, and although her tummy was still a little bigger than she would have liked, the dress fitted beautifully and she wasn't ashamed in any way of her post-pregnancy figure.

'It's lovely, Liz. Are you sure?'

'Of course I'm sure. How about a little pashmina? I've got one that I wear with it to keep the chill off, and it might get cold later.'

She borrowed them both, but stuck to her little flat

black pumps. They had sparkly gems on the toe and they fitted, more to the point.

She showered and then tipped out her bag, hunting through the things she'd thrown into it in haste on the way up, and then wailed.

'What's up?'

Matt appeared in the doorway, and she pulled the borrowed dressing gown tighter round her. 'No knickers.'

'Ah.' He disappeared, and came back a moment later dangling a scrap of cream lace from one finger.

She frowned and snatched them from his fingertip. 'They're mine!'

'Yup. I must have scooped them up with the suit and things the morning after the wedding. I didn't exactly pack carefully.'

'No.' He hadn't. He scooped everything up and shoved it in the bag, and she hadn't been able to find the tiny lace shorts. 'So what are they doing here?'

'They were in my case—in the pocket. I found them and washed them—I meant to give them back to you ages ago, but I shoved them in the case and just forgot. You talking about it reminded me.'

'Thanks. They'll go a treat with the nursing bra.'

He started to laugh, and then he pulled her into his arms and hugged her close, pressing a kiss to her forehead. 'You're gorgeous, Amy. You don't need sexy underwear to turn me on.'

And just like that, with those few words, her body came alive in his arms. Her breath caught in her throat, her heart speeded up, and she took a shaky step back and met his eyes. 'Shoo,' she said, more firmly than she felt. 'I need to feed Josh and express some more milk

before we go, and I don't need an audience. If you want
to do something useful, you can make me a cup of tea.'

He went, humming softly as he walked away, and she
shut the door and put on the little shorts. They looked
all right, she thought, even though she'd gained a little
weight. She'd been too thin at the wedding—worrying
about seeing him again.

Now, she couldn't wait to be alone with him, and
she put on the borrowed makeup—a touch of concealer
over the bags under her eyes from the disturbed nights,
a streak of eyeshadow over her lids, a flick of mascara.
Nothing more. She'd eat the lipstick off in moments, and
anyway Matt didn't like kissing lipstick, and she really,
really hoped he'd end up kissing her goodnight.

At the very least...

'Mr Walker! Welcome back, sir.'

Matt smiled. 'Sorry—wrong Mr Walker. You're
thinking of my twin brother,' he explained with a grin.
'I'm not two-timing Daisy.'

'My apologies, sir—I must say I'm relieved to hear it.'
The maitre d' beamed and showed them to their table,
set in a quiet alcove. 'I've put you at their favourite table.
He caused quite a stir in here the night he proposed to
Mrs Walker. How are they?'

'Very well. They had a boy.'

'Ah. I wondered. Well, please give them our congratulations. May I get you a drink?'

'Yes—thank you. Could we have sparkling water?'

'Of course.'

He faded away, and Amy smiled. 'Don't you ever get
sick of that happening?'

He grinned. 'No, not really. I'm used to it. It's a bit

more complicated when we're working together. We used to wear colour-coded scrubs and shirts to give the staff a clue, but the patients found it confusing.'

'I've never found it confusing.'

'That's because you love me,' he said, and then let his breath out on a sigh and smiled wryly. 'Sorry. Ignore me.'

It was on the tip of her tongue to say yes, he was right, but she didn't, and a waiter appeared with their sparkling water and menus, and they ordered their food. Eventually.

'I can't decide,' she'd said, and he grinned.

'Neither can I. Let's share, then we can have two dishes from each course.'

So they did, swapping plates halfway through, or a little more than half in Matt's case because he was bigger than her and it was only fair, but the food was gorgeous and she was reluctant to let it go.

'I want everything,' she said, and he just laughed and swapped the plates.

'We'll come again,' he said, and she felt a little flutter in her chest.

'Yes, let's.' She looked away to break the tension, and scanned the room with her eyes. 'It's lovely in here, a real find. I can see why Ben and Daisy like it so much.'

'Yes, so can I.'

She sighed softly, her face thoughtful. 'It's so nice being alone with you like this. It seems forever since we did it.'

'It is. The last time we had dinner together was before Samuel.'

She smiled sadly, twisting his heart. 'And all I wanted was peanut butter.'

He nodded. 'I've thought about that. I should have realised at Christmas when you were eating that sandwich.'

'I should have told you. I wanted to, but I was blocking it out, too afraid of what might come out if I let go, and I wanted to protect you, just in case.'

His hand found hers lying on the table, his thumb tracing circles on the soft skin. 'I didn't need protecting, Amy,' he said softly. 'I just needed to share it with you, whatever it was. Promise me you'll never do that again, whatever happens, whatever you're worried about, whatever you're afraid of. Tell me the truth. And I'll do the same. We need to learn to open up to each other, to talk about the things that really matter. And it won't always be easy. It never is, but we have to.'

She nodded. 'I agree.' She hesitated for a moment, then took the first step on that road. 'Can I ask you something about the house?'

He gave a slightly puzzled frown. 'Sure. What about it?'

'Why did you do it like that?'

'Like what?'

'All of it—the kitchen I'd said I liked, the colours, the granite—you even kept the wisteria, and a lawn. We'd talked about needing a lawn for children to play on, although you'd talked about having a modern low-maintenance garden.'

'It is low maintenance. It's mostly paved, and I found I wanted a piece of lawn—just a little bit of home, I suppose,' he said, but then remembered what he'd said about telling the truth, and he smiled wryly. 'And I suppose I hoped that you'd come back to me, that one day we might have another child to play on the lawn. And yeah, I did the kitchen for you, and painted it all for you in your favourite colours. I told you that.'

'But you didn't really say why.'

'For you. I did all of it for you. I wanted you back, Amy, and I still do. I've told you that.'

'You said you wanted me to come and live with you with Josh. I thought—'

She broke off, and he prompted her. 'You thought…?'

'I thought you wanted Josh with you, and it was the easiest way. And the cheapest, if you were talking about paying my rent so I didn't have to worry about money. It would be cheaper and easier and more convenient to have me with you.'

'And you really thought that was why I wanted you to come back to me?' he asked, genuinely shocked. His hand tightened on hers. 'Oh, Amy. I didn't even give the money a thought. I just—it seemed a way to convince you to come back to me. It was nothing to do with Josh, nothing at all. Of course I want to be near him, but I would have moved, would have found a way like Ben did to be near Florence. But I want *you*, Amy. I love you, I always have, I always will, and I don't want to be without you. Josh is amazing, and having him in my life is wonderful, but the thought of my life without you in it is untenable.'

'Really?' She stared at him for ages, and then her eyes filled. 'Oh, Matt. I love you, too. I thought you didn't love me, I thought losing Samuel gave you a way out of a relationship that you hadn't asked for and came to realise you didn't want.'

'Of course I wanted it! Why would I want a way out, Amy? I love you. I'll always love you. I thought four years would be enough to get over you, but I realised at the wedding that I wasn't over you at all, I'd just been marking time.'

'Me, too.' Her smile was gentle, her eyes filled with tears, and suddenly he wanted to be alone with her— completely alone, so he could hold her, touch her, love her.

And lovely though the restaurant was, he'd had enough of it. He glanced up and caught the waiter's eye, and asked for the bill.

'Is everything all right, sir?' he asked worriedly, and Matt smiled.

'Everything's fine. Thank you.'

'Matt?'

He stroked her wrist with his thumb again, tracing the pulse point, feeling it leap. 'I just want to be alone with you,' he said a little gruffly, and her eyes widened slightly. And then she smiled, and ran the tip of her tongue lightly over her lips. He groaned softly and closed his eyes.

'Stop it,' he murmured, as the waiter came back with the bill and the card machine. He didn't even glance at the bill, just keyed in his PIN and left a couple of notes on the table as he ushered Amy out.

They walked to the car in silence, hand in hand, and he drove home as fast as was sensible.

The house was quiet when they got in, a note on the kitchen table. 'All well. Josh is in with us. Sleep well.'

He met her eyes, slid his fingers through hers and led her upstairs to his room. There wasn't a sound in the house except the ticking of the clock, and he closed the door of his room and turned to Amy in the moonlight.

'Come here,' he said gruffly, and wrapped her in his arms, his mouth coming down on hers tentatively, searchingly. He hadn't kissed her since the wedding, not like this, and he wasn't entirely sure of how she'd react. It was still only weeks since Josh's birth, and although she seemed well...

He needn't have worried. She slid her arms around his neck, leant into him and kissed him back with the pent-up longing of all those years without him, and with a groan of satisfaction he let instinct guide him and plundered her mouth with his.

She stopped him after a moment, easing away and looking up at him regretfully. 'Matt, we can't. What if I get pregnant?'

He smiled. 'Don't worry. My brother's a good boy scout. I checked his bedside locker. They've just been to stay.'

'And?'

'And I may have raided it.'

She smiled back, her lips parting on a soft laugh and her eyes creasing. 'Well done,' she said, and went back into his arms.

'So how do you feel about coming back to London to live with me?'

She was propped up against the headboard feeding Joshua, Matt beside her with his arm around her shoulders, and she turned her head and met his eyes.

'It sounds lovely. I'll miss being near Ben and Daisy, but it's not far from them, we can see them often.'

'We can. They're talking of selling both houses and buying something bigger, so we'll be able to go and stay, and I'm sure we can squeeze them in here. And if you really want to work, I'm sure we can find room in the department for another midwife for a few shifts a week—especially if her name's Mrs Walker.'

She went still and searched his eyes. He was smiling, but his eyes were serious and thoughtful. 'I might want to keep my maiden name,' she said, fishing hard because she wasn't quite sure, and the smile spread to his eyes.

'They'll all gossip about us.'

'How will they know?'

'Because I can't keep my hands off you?' he murmured, and she laughed softly.

'Really, Mr Walker, that's so unprofessional.'

'I like to keep tabs on my staff.'

'Well, just make sure you're only keeping those sort of tabs on one member of staff, please,' she scolded, and he chuckled and hugged her closer.

'Absolutely. So—is that a yes?'

'Was that a proposal?'

He smiled wryly. 'I've already asked you once. And I haven't got a ring to give you.'

'I've still got the one you gave me. It's in my jewellery box, with Samuel's scan photo.'

His lips parted, and he let his breath out slowly and hugged her. 'Oh, sweetheart. I thought you would have sold it.'

'Why would I do that?'

He shrugged. 'To fund your trip to India?'

She smiled sadly. 'I could never have sold it, and I didn't need much money in India. All I did was walk along beaches and sleep under the stars and think.'

'On your own? That doesn't sound very safe.'

'I didn't care about safe, Matt, and it didn't cost a lot which was good, because I didn't have much. But I would never have sold your ring. It would be like selling part of myself.'

He picked up her hand, stroking her ring finger softly, his heart pounding. 'Will you wear it for me again?'

'You could ask me again, just so I know you mean it.'

'I just did, and you know I mean it, Amy,' he said, and then gave a rueful laugh and gave up. He wasn't going to get away with it, obviously, but he wasn't going down on one knee. That would mean letting her go and he didn't plan on doing that any time soon, so he shifted so he was facing her, still holding her hand, his eyes locked with hers.

'I love you, my darling, and I want to spend my life with you, and with Josh and any other children that might come along in due course, and I want to grow old with you, so you can trim the hair in my ears and buy me new slippers for Christmas and remind me of where I've left my glasses. So will you marry me? Share your life with me? I'll put your tights on for you when you can't bend over any more, and I promise I won't steal your false teeth.'

She started to laugh, but then her eyes filled with tears and she rested her head on his shoulder and sighed. 'That sounds lovely. So lovely.'

'Even the false teeth and the hair in my ears?' he laughed.

'I'll buy you one of those gadgets. And that's a yes, by the way. I'd love to marry you, as soon as you like, but—can we have a quiet wedding? Just family and a few friends.'

'Sure. Where?'

'Here? In the church where we were going to get

married before? And maybe—if we got married on a Saturday, perhaps we could have Josh christened there on the Sunday, while the others are around?'

'That sounds lovely,' he said softly. 'In fact, if you want, maybe the vicar could say a few words before the service, to remember Samuel.'

Her eyes flooded with tears. 'Oh, yes. Oh, Matt, that would be—'

She broke off and he hugged her. 'Shh. Don't cry any more, my love. It's going to be all right.'

'Yes. Yes, it is.' She looked down at Josh, fast asleep at her breast, and smiled tenderly.

'It's all going to be all right.'

The wedding took place in September, on the anniversary weekend of Ben and Daisy's wedding, in the family's little parish church outside Harrogate. It was decorated with flowers from the lady who'd sold them the posy they'd taken to the cemetery, and it looked lovely.

So did Amy.

She was wearing a simple, elegant cream dress—not a wedding dress, because she'd refused to go down that route, and he hadn't wanted to argue with her. Not about their wedding. All he was doing this time was listening. And when he saw her as she walked towards him on his father's arm, carrying a posy of those lovely, natural flowers, Matt thought he'd never seen anyone more beautiful.

It was a short service, but heartfelt, and afterwards they took everyone to the restaurant for a meal to celebrate.

The staff had opened the restaurant specially for the

afternoon, and it was a meal to remember. They pulled out all the stops, and the food was amazing, but there were not supposed to be any speeches. Matt said he wasn't going to give Ben a chance to get back at him, but there was some good-natured rivalry and a lot of love, and in the end Ben had his way.

'I don't have a lot to say,' he began, which made Matt laugh so hard he had tears running down his face, but Ben waited him out with a patient smile, and then he started again.

'I just wanted to say how much this means to all of us, to see the two of you together again. I'm not going to make any cruel jokes about what a lousy brother you've been, because you haven't. You've supported me through some pretty tough times, and I wish I could have done more for you, but I don't suppose anyone could. However, I can take credit for bringing you together again a year ago tomorrow, even if you didn't appreciate it at the time, and the consequences are delightful!'

At that point Josh gave a shrill squeal and banged his rattle on the table in front of Liz, and everyone laughed.

'So, no bad jokes, just a few words to wish you well, and to say how glad we all are that this day has come for you at last. Ladies and gentlemen, can we please raise our glasses to Matt and Amy!'

'Matt and Amy!' they chorused, and Matt leant over and planted a lingering kiss on her lips. It was full of promise, and the smile in his eyes warmed her to the bottom of her heart.

They went back to the farmhouse for the night. As usual they were in Matt's room with Josh, with Ben and Daisy next door with Thomas, and Amy lay there in Matt's arms in blissful contentment.

'All right, my darling?' he murmured, and she made a soft sound of agreement and snuggled closer.

'It was a lovely day.'

'It was. You looked beautiful in that dress.'

She tipped her head and searched his eyes in the moonlight. 'It was only a simple little shift dress.'

'It was elegant and understated, and you looked amazing.'

She smiled. 'Thank you. You looked pretty amazing yourself, and Josh was so good. I was sure he'd scream all through the service.'

She saw his lips twitch. 'He's probably saving that for tomorrow, for the vicar.'

He wasn't. Josh and his cousin Thomas were both as good as gold for their christening, and the vicar remarked on how alike they were.

'It'll be hard to tell the difference between these two,' he said with a smile as he handed Josh back to Amy.

'No, it won't,' they all chorused, and then laughed. He was right, they were very alike, but there were differences, more so than between Ben and Matt, and to their parents and grandparents the differences were obvious.

They filed out into the sunshine, and Matt and Amy hung back behind the others for a moment, Josh squirming in Matt's arms.

'OK?'

She nodded. 'It was lovely. Just right.'

It had been. Before the ceremony, the vicar who'd married them had asked for a few moments of silence while they remembered Samuel.

They hadn't cried. Their tears had been shed, their love was stronger, and they were looking forward to their future together. It might not be untroubled, but it would be shared every step of the way, and whatever happened, they would always know that they were truly loved.

What more could they possibly ask for?

'Come on, you two, or we'll eat all the cake!' Ben yelled, and Matt laughed.

'He's not joking. Come on.'

And putting his arm round Amy and drawing her in close to his side, he walked her out of the churchyard with a smile...

* * * * *

ROMANCE

The Most Coveted Prize	Penny Jordan
The Costarella Conquest	Emma Darcy
The Night that Changed Everything	Anne McAllister
Craving the Forbidden	India Grey
The Lost Wife	Maggie Cox
Heiress Behind the Headlines	Caitlin Crews
Weight of the Crown	Christina Hollis
Innocent in the Ivory Tower	Lucy Ellis
Flirting With Intent	Kelly Hunter
A Moment on the Lips	Kate Hardy
Her Italian Soldier	Rebecca Winters
The Lonesome Rancher	Patricia Thayer
Nikki and the Lone Wolf	Marion Lennox
Mardie and the City Surgeon	Marion Lennox
Bridesmaid Says, 'I Do!'	Barbara Hannay
The Princess Test	Shirley Jump
Breaking Her No-Dates Rule	Emily Forbes
Waking Up With Dr Off-Limits	Amy Andrews

HISTORICAL

The Lady Forfeits	Carole Mortimer
Valiant Soldier, Beautiful Enemy	Diane Gaston
Winning the War Hero's Heart	Mary Nichols
Hostage Bride	Anne Herries

MEDICAL ROMANCE™

Tempted by Dr Daisy	Caroline Anderson
The Fiancée He Can't Forget	Caroline Anderson
A Cotswold Christmas Bride	Joanna Neil
All She Wants For Christmas	Annie Claydon

0911 GEN STD HB

ROMANCE

Passion and the Prince	Penny Jordan
For Duty's Sake	Lucy Monroe
Alessandro's Prize	Helen Bianchin
Mr and Mischief	Kate Hewitt
Her Desert Prince	Rebecca Winters
The Boss's Surprise Son	Teresa Carpenter
Ordinary Girl in a Tiara	Jessica Hart
Tempted by Trouble	Liz Fielding

HISTORICAL

Secret Life of a Scandalous Debutante	Bronwyn Scott
One Illicit Night	Sophia James
The Governess and the Sheikh	Marguerite Kaye
Pirate's Daughter, Rebel Wife	June Francis

MEDICAL ROMANCE™

Taming Dr Tempest	Meredith Webber
The Doctor and the Debutante	Anne Fraser
The Honourable Maverick	Alison Roberts
The Unsung Hero	Alison Roberts
St Piran's: The Fireman and Nurse Loveday	Kate Hardy
From Brooding Boss to Adoring Dad	Dianne Drake

Mills & Boon® Hard Back

November 2011

ROMANCE

The Power of Vasilii	Penny Jordan
The Real Rio D'Aquila	Sandra Marton
A Shameful Consequence	Carol Marinelli
A Dangerous Infatuation	Chantelle Shaw
Kholodov's Last Mistress	Kate Hewitt
His Christmas Acquisition	Cathy Williams
The Argentine's Price	Maisey Yates
Captive but Forbidden	Lynn Raye Harris
On the First Night of Christmas...	Heidi Rice
The Power and the Glory	Kimberly Lang
How a Cowboy Stole Her Heart	Donna Alward
Tall, Dark, Texas Ranger	Patricia Thayer
The Secretary's Secret	Michelle Douglas
Rodeo Daddy	Soraya Lane
The Boy is Back in Town	Nina Harrington
Confessions of a Girl-Next-Door	Jackie Braun
Mistletoe, Midwife...Miracle Baby	Anne Fraser
Dynamite Doc or Christmas Dad?	Marion Lennox

HISTORICAL

The Lady Confesses	Carole Mortimer
The Dangerous Lord Darrington	Sarah Mallory
The Unconventional Maiden	June Francis
Her Battle-Scarred Knight	Meriel Fuller

MEDICAL ROMANCE™

The Child Who Rescued Christmas	Jessica Matthews
Firefighter With A Frozen Heart	Dianne Drake
How to Save a Marriage in a Million	Leonie Knight
Swallowbrook's Winter Bride	Abigail Gordon

Mills & Boon® Large Print

November 2011

ROMANCE

HISTORICAL

MEDICAL ROMANCE™